SHADOWSEER: ATHENS

(SHADOWSEER, BOOK FIVE)

MORGAN RICE

Morgan Rice

Morgan Rice is the #1 bestselling and USA Today bestselling author of the epic fantasy series THE SORCERER'S RING, comprising seventeen books; of the #1 bestselling series THE VAMPIRE JOURNALS, comprising twelve books; of the #1 bestselling series THE SURVIVAL TRILOGY, a post-apocalyptic thriller comprising three books; of the epic fantasy series KINGS AND SORCERERS, comprising six books; of the epic fantasy series OF CROWNS AND GLORY, comprising eight books; of the epic fantasy series A THRONE FOR SISTERS, comprising eight books; of the science fiction series THE INVASION CHRONICLES, comprising four books; of the fantasy series OLIVER BLUE AND THE SCHOOL FOR SEERS, comprising four books; of the fantasy series THE WAY OF STEEL, comprising four books; of the fantasy series AGE OF THE SORCERERS, comprising eight books; and of the new fantasy series SHADOWSEER, comprising five books. Morgan's books are available in audio and print editions, and translations are available in over 25 languages.

Morgan loves to hear from you, so please feel free to visit www.morganricebooks.com to join the email list, receive a free book, receive free giveaways, download the free app, get the latest exclusive news, connect on Facebook and Twitter, and stay in touch!

ISBN: 978-1-0943-7702-5

Select Acclaim for Morgan Rice

"If you thought that there was no reason left for living after the end of THE SORCERER'S RING series, you were wrong. In RISE OF THE DRAGONS Morgan Rice has come up with what promises to be another brilliant series, immersing us in a fantasy of trolls and dragons, of valor, honor, courage, magic and faith in your destiny. Morgan has managed again to produce a strong set of characters that make us cheer for them on every page....Recommended for the permanent library of all readers that love a well-written fantasy."
--*Books and Movie Reviews*
Roberto Mattos

"An action packed fantasy sure to please fans of Morgan Rice's previous novels, along with fans of works such as THE INHERITANCE CYCLE by Christopher Paolini.... Fans of Young Adult Fiction will devour this latest work by Rice and beg for more."
--*The Wanderer, A Literary Journal* (regarding *Rise of the Dragons*)

"A spirited fantasy that weaves elements of mystery and intrigue into its story line. *A Quest of Heroes* is all about the making of courage and about realizing a life purpose that leads to growth, maturity, and excellence....For those seeking meaty fantasy adventures, the protagonists, devices, and action provide a vigorous set of encounters that focus well on Thor's evolution from a dreamy child to a young adult facing impossible odds for survival....Only the beginning of what promises to be an epic young adult series."
--*Midwest Book Review* (D. Donovan, eBook Reviewer)

"THE SORCERER'S RING has all the ingredients for an instant success: plots, counterplots, mystery, valiant knights, and blossoming relationships replete with broken hearts, deception and betrayal. It will keep you entertained for hours, and will satisfy all ages. Recommended for the permanent library of all fantasy readers."
--*Books and Movie Reviews*, Roberto Mattos

"In this action-packed first book in the epic fantasy Sorcerer's Ring series (which is currently 14 books strong), Rice introduces readers to 14-year-old Thorgrin "Thor" McLeod, whose dream is to join the Silver

Legion, the elite knights who serve the king.... Rice's writing is solid and the premise intriguing."
  --*Publishers Weekly*

A DIRGE FOR PRINCES (Book #4)
A JEWEL FOR ROYALS (BOOK #5)
A KISS FOR QUEENS (BOOK #6)
A CROWN FOR ASSASSINS (Book #7)
A CLASP FOR HEIRS (Book #8)

OF CROWNS AND GLORY
SLAVE, WARRIOR, QUEEN (Book #1)
ROGUE, PRISONER, PRINCESS (Book #2)
KNIGHT, HEIR, PRINCE (Book #3)
REBEL, PAWN, KING (Book #4)
SOLDIER, BROTHER, SORCERER (Book #5)
HERO, TRAITOR, DAUGHTER (Book #6)
RULER, RIVAL, EXILE (Book #7)
VICTOR, VANQUISHED, SON (Book #8)

KINGS AND SORCERERS
RISE OF THE DRAGONS (Book #1)
RISE OF THE VALIANT (Book #2)
THE WEIGHT OF HONOR (Book #3)
A FORGE OF VALOR (Book #4)
A REALM OF SHADOWS (Book #5)
NIGHT OF THE BOLD (Book #6)

THE SORCERER'S RING
A QUEST OF HEROES (Book #1)
A MARCH OF KINGS (Book #2)
A FATE OF DRAGONS (Book #3)
A CRY OF HONOR (Book #4)
A VOW OF GLORY (Book #5)
A CHARGE OF VALOR (Book #6)
A RITE OF SWORDS (Book #7)
A GRANT OF ARMS (Book #8)
A SKY OF SPELLS (Book #9)
A SEA OF SHIELDS (Book #10)
A REIGN OF STEEL (Book #11)
A LAND OF FIRE (Book #12)
A RULE OF QUEENS (Book #13)
AN OATH OF BROTHERS (Book #14)
A DREAM OF MORTALS (Book #15)
A JOUST OF KNIGHTS (Book #16)

THE GIFT OF BATTLE (Book #17)

THE SURVIVAL TRILOGY
ARENA ONE: SLAVERSUNNERS (Book #1)
ARENA TWO (Book #2)
ARENA THREE (Book #3)

VAMPIRE, FALLEN
BEFORE DAWN (Book #1)

THE VAMPIRE JOURNALS
TURNED (Book #1)
LOVED (Book #2)
BETRAYED (Book #3)
DESTINED (Book #4)
DESIRED (Book #5)
BETROTHED (Book #6)
VOWED (Book #7)
FOUND (Book #8)
RESURRECTED (Book #9)
CRAVED (Book #10)
FATED (Book #11)
OBSESSED (Book #12)

Want free books?

Subscribe to Morgan Rice's email list and receive 4 free books, 3 free maps, 1 free app, 1 free game, 1 free graphic novel, and exclusive giveaways! To subscribe, visit: www.morganricebooks.com

CHAPTER ONE

There was a shadow here somewhere. Nasos had felt it. They all had.

Nasos crept on silent feet with the other shadowseers through the back streets of Athens, his group moving in careful concert as they hunted for a shadow. Each of them looked around carefully, watching for any sign.

He passed by a broadsheet seller and stepped around a horse and cart, keeping his eyes on the others. The presence of the Acropolis stood far above, a reminder of Greece's ancient past even in the modern world of 1858. It was also what he and the others were there to protect.

He wondered what they must look like to any of the natives of the city who glanced out of their windows as they passed, this group of a dozen men and women combing the streets, trying to use senses most people didn't have to locate a creature that most people wouldn't have believed existed.

Would they even spot that they were a group? They weren't dressed the same, each wearing whatever they felt was easiest to move in and pass for normal in. Yes, most of the clothes were darker to allow them to pass unnoticed at night, although it was day now, and *all* of them had more pouches and pockets than anyone normally needed, the better to hold weapons, but it wasn't as if they wore a uniform for this.

Nasos was wearing a simple open-necked peasant shirt and loose trousers, held up with a belt that had pouches set around it to hold everything he might need in the hunt for a shadow. He was only average height, slender and wiry, his body hardened by the training, his dark hair cropped short, his brown eyes darting around to check for danger.

The heat of the noonday sun beat down on the city, making its white walls gleam, the marble of its ruins seeming almost to shine with reflected glory. Nasos had been brought up in Thessalonica, though, and he was more than used to the heat. He took comfort in it. It was far better to take on a shadow in the daylight than in the darkness. There was nowhere for it to hide in the daylight.

"Keep up," Andreas said. "And stop daydreaming. We've work to do."

Nasos bit back his frustration at the words. Because he was only eighteen, the youngest of those there, everyone seemed to think that they could tell him what to do. They acted as if he hadn't undergone the same training they had to be a shadowseer, hadn't worked on the small flicker of talent he possessed just as hard, hadn't faced the same dangers.

Of course, he *hadn't* faced as many of them as some of the others. Dias, for example, was nearly fifty, and had been fighting against the shadows for most of his life, defending Athens and the ritual site there from any incursion. He moved with the wary expertise of someone who had seen many battles, checking every door they passed, scanning the flat rooftops of the houses for dangers.

Lucretia had scars along her arms from battles against some of those who had been possessed. She wore her weapons easily, hands resting only inches from the grips of them. She slipped through a gap between two pedestrians as smoothly as a dancer.

Ten others moved in concert, each a well-trained part of a single whole, each one of their dozen dangerous in their own right, but far more capable together.

Nasos wasn't the strongest of them, but he could hold his own. He could fight, and he could sneak through the world without being seen. He did it now, slipping from hiding place to hiding place as he moved forward.

He leapt over a low wall, clambered up the side of a building, then down the other, following after the rest of the shadowseers. He could feel the presence of the shadows, and with the others there, would perform the exorcisms that drove them from a body.

He reminded himself of all of that as he followed the others, but still, he was nervous as their group made its way through the city, the twelve spreading out in twos and threes, following the feeling of one of the shadows there, tracking it the way a hunter might have tracked the spoor of an animal. Being nervous was good though. Shadows were dangerous, even when there was a whole group of shadowseers to face them.

They came out into a small cobbled square with a fountain at its heart depicting Psyche and Eros. The houses that formed its sides were large, square things, designed to keep the heat inside from becoming too oppressive.

2

There was a figure sitting on the side of the fountain, a dark-haired young woman in a simple white dress that made her look like something out of a myth, dangling her legs over the side of the fountain and kicking them casually, as if she hadn't a care in the world.

Nasos wasn't fooled. He could feel the shadow in her even from where she stood, with no attempt on the creature's part to hide it, none of their usual tricks that held back what they were until one was almost on top of them.

Instead, the darkness in her shone out, whispering with power and danger. It was like… like a beacon. Like a lighthouse drawing them in. Or like a wrecker's light, trying to draw a ship onto the rocks.

The dozen shadowseers spread out around her, hemming her in, leaving her no way to escape.

"This is wrong," Nasos said to Andreas. "It's too easy."

"Easy is good," Andreas replied, with a note of impatience. "We have the thing trapped. Out here, with so much light around, it has nowhere to jump except under the fountain. We can contain it when we drive it out."

"It isn't polite to talk about someone without addressing them," the young woman said. She stopped dangling her feet in the fountain and stepped down to stand in the square opposite Nasos and the others, smiling as she did so.

Nasos found himself hanging back when he knew he should have been moving forward. Something was wrong here. Something was *very* wrong.

"Leave that body," Andreas said. "Do it in peace, or we will drive you out by force."

"No, I don't think I will," the woman said. "As hateful as the form and order of your world are, I must admit that there are so many fascinating pleasures that can only be experienced with a corporeal form. And, of course, I have tasks to perform that require it."

Andreas was as steadfast and unyielding as always, giving no ground, not even for an instant. Nasos could only admire that about him. It was just… he felt certain that there was more going on here. The shadow was too confident for someone who was surrounded.

"Whatever your plans in this city," Andreas said, "they will not come to fruition. We will stop you."

The woman smiled then, as if she found the whole thing funny beyond words. "Oh, I would like to see you try. But as for *my* plans, do you think I'm here alone?"

3

Nasos felt the moment when the presence of other shadows flared more strongly all around him. Figures started to step from the doorways of the houses around them, men and women, young and old, all possessed, all with the power of the shadows running through them. All of them carried weapons, some with knives, some with clubs, a couple with pistols that made even the smallest of them deadly. He knew then that this had been a trap from the start, that they'd been lured there specifically for this.

"We knew you were in the city," the woman said, as her fellow shadows spread out around the shadowseers. "And our work at the Acropolis is too important to be disturbed by you."

"The Acropolis?" Nasos said. "But that… that's where the ritual takes place."

The ritual that had been designed by the first shadowseers. The one that had banished shadows from the world before, using the shadowseers' most potent relic, the one crafted by the twins who had fought back against the rule of the shadows. The one that had cost the lives of those performing it, none of the pairs of twins undertaking it quite powerful enough to destroy the shadows once and for all.

The whole point of the shadowseers here was to keep shadows away from the ritual site, to keep it open in case it ever needed to be used again. It was their sacred duty.

"Of course," the woman said. "Every inch of it was worked to focus power. But that power can be turned to other purposes just as easily."

"What purpose?" Andreas demanded.

For a moment, Nasos thought the shadow might continue talking but instead, she shrugged.

"Enough talk, I think," she said, in a slightly bored tone. She waved a hand almost negligently at the shadowseers. "We cannot have them stopping us. Kill them."

The possessed figures charged forward, weapons raised, and Nasos braced himself for a fight. Even as he did it, he felt Andreas's hands on him, pushing him away.

"Run, Nasos! Get clear! Warn the others about what has happened here!"

Nasos didn't want to run. He wanted to stay, he wanted to fight. He wanted to defend the others with whom he'd spent so much time fighting against the evil that threatened to overwhelm the world.

Andreas shoved him again, though, and Nasos found that another part of him wanted to survive. He ran without thinking, even as shots sounded behind him. Something flew past his head, and the bullet took a splinter from a house in front of Nasos. One of the shadow possessed stepped into his path, swinging a knife, and it was all Nasos could do to dodge out of the way and keep moving.

Around him, he saw the others fighting the shadow possessed, striking out with fists and feet, drawing an array of weapons so that blades struck against blades, clubs lashed out to crack against limbs. The shadowseers had all the skills that came from years of training, all the specialized skills that were designed to take on shadows who possessed people. For a moment, Nasos dared to believe that maybe they might come through this.

Then he saw the woman who had been sitting on the fountain pick up Andreas as easily as if he were a child, the shadow within her lending her strength, or perhaps just giving her access to all the potential strength that her body held. She lifted him up over her head like some kind of offering to the gods of Ancient Greece…

Then she brought him down across her knee with a sickening crack as his spine snapped, his body broken with brutal force. Nasos saw another shadowseer gutted by a knife in a spray of blood, and a third brought down by a pistol fired at point-blank range.

The sheer horror of everything going on around him paralyzed Nasos, and in that moment, another of the shadow possessed came at him with a blade. Nasos twisted aside, but it still cut across his side.

The pain of it snapped him out of his immobility. Nasos struck out with the palm of his hand, slamming it into his foe's jaw. He tripped the possessed man with one foot, then kicked him in the face to send him sprawling.

Nasos was running again then, ducking and dodging as more shots sounded behind him. His arm swept out, knocking the contents of a fruit stall into the street as he passed, trying to slow down those who followed him at least a little. He took turnings at random through the city, ignoring the looks he got from people all around. He could hear footsteps following, could feel the presence of the shadows, but he didn't dare look behind.

He took another turning, scrambled up a low wall, and leapt down the other side. That bought him a moment or two, and he dove through an open window on the ground floor of a taverna, plunging through the building as rapidly as he could. He came out of the other side and kept running.

There were no footsteps behind him now, and he couldn't feel the shadows. Now, Nasos dared to look behind him. There was no one there, no one following. Even so, he took a few more turnings, wanting to make sure that he wouldn't be found. Finally, he huddled down in a doorway, feeling the terror and the pain wash over him now that the adrenaline of the chase was gone.

He put his hand to his side. It came away slick with blood, but at least he was alive. Would any of the others have made it? He wanted to believe that they might, but honestly, he couldn't see how they could have.

The shadows had killed them, and now they were going to do far worse. Nasos had to get the word out. He had to wire a message to as many other groups of shadowseers as he could. He had to tell someone what the shadows were plotting in Athens before it was too late.

CHAPTER TWO

Kaia wasn't sure that she'd ever looked forward to anything as much as the moment that her sister's carriage came into view out on the outskirts of Rome, rumbling closer to her little by little. Almost all the time that she'd been in the city, separated from her sister, she'd found herself missing Em, and now they were about to meet again.

She stood out there, short and blonde haired, with deep blue eyes and a heart-shaped face, wearing a simple traveling dress that was still richer than anything she'd owned growing up in an orphanage. She was slightly tanned now by the Mediterranean sun, her hair bleached even lighter by it.

Kaia could already hear her sister's voice in her head. That had come back to her the moment Em got near to the city. Kaia had never felt so alone as when Em's voice had faded when her aunt had separated them, making Em go off to Venice without the rest of them. The return of that voice now was like being hugged tight, her presence there palpable.

Almost there now. I've so much to tell you about Venice, Em sent. *Did you find the relic?*

We did, Kaia replied. Not that anything was that simple. *But we need to talk about that. Aunt Keris told me something you need to hear.*

Her aunt was standing beside her, waiting along with her. She was a slender woman in her forties, with a strength and flexibility to her. She kept her blonde hair tied back, and was dressed in dark trousers along with a shapeless top that let her move freely.

Inspector Pinsley was beside her. The inspector was a tall, slender man with aquiline features framed by mutton chop whiskers. He stood ramrod straight as always, as if on parade in his former life as a soldier. His eyes moved constantly, as if looking out for criminals who might wander into his path.

His daughter Olivia stood a couple of paces further away. She was a couple of years older than Kaia and Em's seventeen, a little taller than Kaia, her dark hair tied back in a braid, with features that were a little more delicate than her father's, but still with that same leanness.

What is it? Em asked. *You feel... worried.*

There was no time to explain it all, though, no time to tell her sister what their aunt had explained: that the orb they'd found in Rome was the focal point for a ritual that successive pairs of shadowseer twins had undertaken, trying to drive the shadows from the world.

That they had all died attempting it, succeeding in no more than pushing the shadows back from the world for a while.

Kaia still didn't know how to process that, or what to think about the fact that her aunt had hidden the information from her in a supposed effort to protect her and Em. There was a lot of pain that came from that news, and from how little her aunt had told her.

I... I'll explain it to you when you're here, Kaia promised.

That took only a few more seconds of waiting. Em's carriage pulled up in front of their little group, and almost as soon as it came to a halt, the door flew open, letting Em throw herself out of it, sweeping Kaia into a tight hug. For all the poise and etiquette her sister might have been taught at a finishing school as a ward of the British ambassador to France, she was still far quicker than Kaia to show her emotions.

"It's so good to see you," Em whispered. "I am *never* leaving you again."

Kaia felt exactly the same way when it came to her sister. She'd been conflicted before, because of the way her sister had killed a Catalan prince who had threatened their lives back in Munich, but having to spend so long away from her had shown Kaia just how much she needed her sister beside her.

"Do the rest of us get to join that hug?" Olivia asked, wrapping her arms around the pair of them.

Even as she did it, a second figure got down from the carriage: a young man of about her age whom Kaia recognized as one of the shadowseers who had gone with Em. He was broad shouldered and had sandy blond hair, a square jaw, and handsome features. Kaia saw her aunt look at him with a frown.

"Casper," she said. "Where are the others?"

Kaia saw the worried look that came over the young shadowseer. He shook his head solemnly, a pained expression on his face.

"We walked into an ambush in Venice," he said. "Shadows killed the mask maker. Emmeline and I were the only survivors."

We had to put on masks and hide in a group of dancers, Em sent over to Kaia. *Then we had to try to find the relic on the Rialto Bridge. We had to fight shadows to do it, but it... it was a fake.*

Ours isn't, Kaia replied. *I've felt it. I've used it.*

She'd used it to close a portal beneath Rome, destroying the shadows that had been pouring out of it. The energy of that moment had been greater than anything Kaia had possessed before.

Where is it now? Em asked.

Aunt Keris has it, Kaia replied. *She says that it's too dangerous for me to hold onto.*

"Can I see the relic?" Em asked aloud, as direct as always. Their aunt looked over at the sisters.

"I don't think that's a good idea, girls."

"Please," Em said, obviously not willing to let go of the subject. "After everything that happened, I think I deserve to see it."

Aunt Keris looked as though she might argue, but to Kaia's surprise, she relented, taking the orb out from one of her pockets. It was slightly larger than her hand, made from complex, interlocking swirls of what looked like gold and silver that caught the sunlight and seemed to amplify it, shifting even as Kaia looked.

Em reached out for it, and Kaia saw that glow intensify, just slightly, but Aunt Keris pulled it back.

"I don't think that's such a good idea," she said.

"Why not?" Emmeline asked.

Kaia saw her aunt hesitate, but she wasn't about to allow that. Her sister, her *twin*, had as much right to know about what was going on as Kaia did. This affected her just as much as it did Kaia.

"If you don't tell her, I will," Kaia said.

"Tell her what?" the inspector asked. He might be able to deduce most things, but he hadn't heard any of this, and it wasn't the kind of thing he could just work out.

Aunt Keris looked suddenly conflicted. Then she nodded sharply.

"You're right," she said. "I should tell her. I should tell you all."

"Tell us all what, Keris?" the inspector asked.

Kaia heard her aunt sigh. "The relic is an object of power, one created long ago by a pair of twins in an effort to drive the shadows from the world once and for all. This was during the first war against them, when the shadows ruled much of the world. At least, that is what our histories say."

"The first twins," Casper said, in a slightly awed tone, as if they were part of a legend that he'd heard all his life. Maybe he had. Kaia guessed that the shadowseers had whole histories that she and her sister had never had a chance to hear, since their parents had died trying to draw shadows away from them when they were just babies.

Aunt Keris nodded, and kept going. "They succeeded in pushing out most of the shadows, but the effort... it was too much for them. It cost them their lives, and the shadows were still able to come back."

"So, what are you saying?" Em asked.

"I'm not done," their aunt said, the pain in her voice still obvious. "There have been pairs of twins since. They have always had power, much more than most shadowseers, and together, they have been even more powerful. Each time, they thought that they might be able to succeed where the first twins failed. Each time, they have gone to Athens. Each time, they have attempted the ritual, and each time, they have failed, perishing in the attempt."

That was news that had felt like an utter betrayal when Kaia had heard it less than an hour ago. It meant that her aunt had been pushing her toward the relic, in the full knowledge of what it might do to her and Em if they found it. At the same time, though, it explained some of why she'd wanted to keep the two of them apart. It explained why she'd been so worried about the two of them displaying power, and why she'd tried to keep the orb out of Kaia's hands since they found it.

Kaia didn't have to look at Em's face to know how upset she was in that moment. She could *feel* it.

"So you took us on this whole quest to find this orb of yours, knowing all the while that it might kill us?" Em said. "You failed to mention to us that your endgame in all of this was for us to sacrifice our *lives*?"

She took a step toward Aunt Keris, and Kaia found herself suddenly worried for her aunt's safety. Yes, Aunt Keris had far more experience of violence and the skills associated with it, but Kaia could feel her sister's anger in that moment. So much of it that Kaia felt as though she had to stand in the way, just to make sure nothing bad happened.

Casper stepped in the way, putting his hands on Em's shoulders, and to Kaia's surprise, she didn't shove him aside.

"Em, please," he said.

"I thought that we might be able to make use of the orb without you having to do the ritual," Aunt Keris said. "I thought... I am a shadowseer, Emmeline! I have duties to the world, as well as to my family."

"Duties that include sacrificing us?" Em asked, still not sounding remotely happy. Kaia was still worried about what she might do next.

"Emmeline, that isn't fair," the inspector said, stepping in. "Your aunt has already said that she doesn't want you to complete this ritual, and if I understand it correctly, it is something that takes place in a specific spot?"

"In Athens," Aunt Keris said. "In the Acropolis."

"Then neither of you have to go there," Inspector Pinsley said. "Kaia, I have seen what you can do with that orb. So we take it, and we go elsewhere. You and your sister can still do a considerable amount of good wherever you go, without having to endanger yourselves. You don't have to go anywhere near Athens."

Now, Kaia could feel the nervousness coming off her sister like morning mist. She could feel the fear there through the link the two of them shared.

What is it? she asked.

Before Em could reply, Casper spoke. He looked nervous as he looked across to Em, as if his biggest worry in all of this was that he might upset her.

"That is where we may have a problem," he said. "A big one."

Aunt Keris looked over at him sharply. "What *kind* of problem?"

"On the way over here, I checked some of the message drops," Casper said. "There was an urgent message there. One of our groups has lost contact. Twelve of them, wiped out. The message said they were going to intercept a shadow, but there has been nothing since."

Aunt Keris paled. Kaia got the impression that having so many shadowseers disappear at once wasn't usual. That it was a major event for the shadowseers.

"Where?" her aunt asked.

Casper hesitated only for a moment or two before he answered. "In Athens."

Kaia could see the fear in her aunt as Casper said that.

"No, we can't. We can't go near there."

"We have to, Keris," Casper said. "We have to know what happened. We have to help the one who got the news out."

"We can't," Aunt Keris said.

Kaia could understand her aunt's fear, and she felt a little better of Aunt Keris for it. That hesitation suggested that she did care, at least a little, about what happened to her and Em.

"We could still go," Kaia suggested, knowing that her aunt didn't want to be the one to say it.

What are you doing? Em asked.

"We could still go," Kaia repeated.

"Kaia," Inspector Pinsley said. "It wouldn't be safe."

Kaia shook her head. "Aunt Keris said herself that these twins died when they did this ritual of hers. So we don't do the ritual. No one can make us do it. It's that simple."

Nothing is that simple, Em insisted, inside her mind. Kaia could sense the disapproval there.

They can't make us do anything we don't want to, Kaia argued. *You said that everyone was killed in Venice. If more shadowseers have been killed in Athens, and we can help, shouldn't we?*

"Kaia, we can find another way," Aunt Keris said. She didn't sound convinced, though.

"I don't think there is another way," Casper said. "We are the closest, Keris, and if there *are* shadows there, the relic might give us a chance against them. You know that the shadowseers there protect the ritual site. If shadows are *there*, then we risk losing control of it."

Kaia saw her aunt bow her head.

"You're right."

Keris looked over at the inspector, as if he were the one she had to convince, not the twins. "We can do some good in Athens, and we don't have to perform the ritual. But we can't let the shadows have the city, and we can't let the deaths of so many shadowseers stand. We don't even have to go near the Acropolis. I think... I think we have to go to Athens and find out what happened."

CHAPTER THREE

Kaia stared out of the carriage as they headed west trying to get to the coast, wondering all the while if they were doing the right thing. Should they really be heading for Athens when that was the place the ritual took place, the place that might kill both her and her sister?

Kaia had to remind herself that no one was forcing them to do the ritual. They were going to Athens specifically to try to deal with whatever threat had resulted in the death of a dozen shadowseers, although that was more than terrifying enough. There were only half a dozen of them in the carriage, and only her aunt and Casper truly had the training that shadowseers received. How were they supposed to deal with something that had killed twice as many fully trained shadowseers?

They would find a way. They had to. They couldn't let the shadows do whatever they wanted.

With six of them crammed into the carriage, it was pretty cramped, but at least they were making good time. Kaia could see the coast coming into view now, a shimmer of blue in the distance. The carriage was heading for a small fishing town, tiny compared to some of the cities that Kaia had seen on her travels across Europe.

It seemed strange to her that she should have gotten to see quite so many places as she had. Visiting the likes of Paris, Rome, and Munich was the kind of thing that only the very wealthiest got to do under normal circumstances, yet Kaia, an orphan from south of the Thames in London, had somehow been able to see them all. It was the kind of thing she wouldn't even have dared to dream of doing when she was younger.

Of course, she'd also found herself caught up in murders and in plots to unleash the evils of the shadows onto the world. She'd found herself in incredible danger. She'd found herself having to fight with powers that it seemed on one else possessed to quite the same degree. Not even her own twin sister.

Em was seated opposite her, next to Casper. She could see Em's hand just lightly brushing Casper's, in a way that could have been seen as accidental, if Kaia couldn't feel everything Em felt in that moment.

Kaia could feel the whirl of her thoughts, how upset and confused she still was by everything their aunt had said.

I can't believe that Aunt Keris didn't tell us about the ritual and the danger of it earlier, Em sent, the anger there obvious to Kaia.

I can, Kaia replied. *She has been a shadowseer all her life, trained to fight against the shadows. She has fought against them longer than either of us. And when we started looking for the relic, she didn't know either of us, not really. But she still tried to protect us.*

Is that what you call forcing us to be apart? Sending me into danger in Venice?

Kaia could feel the hurt in her sister's thoughts. How much of it was just because she'd been the one forced to split from the others? How much of it was for the same reason that Kaia felt hurt: because they'd found their remaining family, only for their aunt to hold back information?

I think it was her way of trying, Kaia sent. *She knew that the ritual would require our combined powers, and that we would be targets until then too, so keeping us apart may have seemed like the right thing to do.*

I still don't like it, Em replied. She didn't let the hurt show on her face, but Kaia could still feel it deep within her, like a wound that wouldn't go away.

"What are you two plotting?" Olivia asked. "I can always tell when you start talking to one another without talking. You start staring at one another strangely."

It was strange, how quickly Olivia had come to accept all the strangeness in the world.

"We're not plotting anything," Em said. "I'm just glad to see Kaia again. To see all of you."

"Well, we're glad to see you too, Em," Olivia said, reaching out to take Em's hand. "It will be good to travel with you again."

I wish we were traveling back to Paris, Em sent, *or even over to London. And this business with not letting us near the relic. We're the ones who can use it, right?*

I think any shadowseer can, Kaia explained, *but it reacted far more to me than to Aunt Keris. I used it to close a portal under Rome.*

Then we should be the ones using it, Em sent. *Why go to all the trouble of getting the relic, if we're not going to have access to it? Unless Aunt Keris is lying and she means to make us do this ritual of hers.*

I really don't think she would do that, Kaia insisted.

We'll see.

They arrived in the small fishing town, driving down cobbled streets to the docks. Kaia got out and had to stand there while the inspector and her aunt negotiated in rapid-fire Italian with the captain of a boat, who seemed to be shaking his head at the prospect of taking them all the way across the Ionian and Mediterranean seas to get to Athens.

Then Aunt Keris started to count out money into his hand, probably more than he'd seen before. Certainly enough that after a few seconds of it, he started to nod.

And our aunt gets her way again, Em sent. She didn't sound happy about it at all.

She's not a bad person, Kaia insisted.

She's still not the right person to hold onto the relic.

Was that what a part of this was about?

Kaia shrugged and switched to a whisper. "It's not as if we can do anything about that, Em. It's not as if we can just steal it from her."

Em turned to her with a smile Kaia had started to get to know when it came to her sister; the one that promised trouble.

"Can't we?"

*

Kaia hadn't been on a boat since the journey from England to France, what seemed like a lifetime ago now. Since then, she'd been traveling by trains and carriages, and Kaia had gotten used to them, but not yet to boats. This boat was a little larger than the tiny fishing vessel that had carried her and the inspector on their journey to get to Paris, big enough that it had cabins, big enough that it was possible to walk around the deck for exercise as it continued across the sea between Rome and Greece.

It still felt tiny and insignificant against the vastness of the water, though. That seemed to stretch out all around them, land long out of sight on every side. There was nothing to do right then except to wait for their arrival in Athens and, perhaps, to worry about what her sister was planning to do next.

Em was out on the deck, currently talking to the young shadowseer who had come with her from Venice, Casper. They were holding hands, and she was smiling as she talked to him, leaning in close. Olivia was up there too, and Kaia had the feeling that she had appointed herself as a kind of chaperone, or perhaps been appointed as such by the inspector. He and Aunt Keris were somewhere below together, possibly talking about the current situation, possibly simply getting to know one another better, possibly doing more. They hadn't exactly tried to hide how fascinating each found the other since they'd met back in Munich, or the sparks of romance that both of them seemed too straight-laced and English to actually show.

Kaia saw Em and Casper split, each walking in a different direction as if the boat were big enough for anyone to truly be apart. She saw the way Em watched the boy go.

"So, you like him?" Kaia asked.

"Don't be silly, he's really irritating," Em replied, a fraction too fast, in Kaia's opinion.

Kaia cocked her head to one side. "You know I can feel what you're feeling?"

"I'm not feeling anything about Casper. He's just some boy who *happened* to be there in Venice. That's all."

Kaia wondered if her sister actually believed that. *She* certainly didn't, not with the way they looked at one another.

"Look, forget Casper," Em said. Did Kaia see her flush slightly as she said his name? Normally, her sister was so poised, so in control, and she certainly didn't react like that around a boy. "I want to talk about what we discussed before, on the docks."

"What we discussed?" Kaia said.

Stealing back the relic, Em sent.

Wait, you're serious about that? Kaia replied. It was hard to believe that her sister might actually mean it. But then, this was Em, and she had a long history of doing things that were a lot more direct and impulsive than anything Kaia might do, however much the two of them might look the same.

It's not right that Aunt Keris holds onto it, when we're the ones who can use it best, Em sent. *It's not right that she should just get to control everything about all this. So I think that we should go get it. It's in her cabin, I'm sure of it. And she is currently in the* inspector's *cabin, talking.*

You want to do this now? Kaia asked, scarcely able to believe it.

There might not be another chance.

Em headed belowdecks, and Kaia found herself following in her sister's wake, more to try to find a way to keep Em out of trouble than because she thought any of this was a good idea. They reached the cabins, pausing at the door to the inspector's. Kaia could hear the

16

murmur of voices and recognized her aunt's even though she couldn't make out the words.

Her cabin really was empty, and Em was already taking advantage of that fact, moving to it and going inside. Kaia followed and found her sister starting to search the few belongings that Aunt Keris had brought along with her, going through her bags.

"Em, I really don't feel comfortable about this," she said. "We shouldn't be going through Aunt Keris's things. Especially not for the orb."

"If we don't have it, then we can't fight against the shadows," Em said. "I saw what they could do back in Munich. They... they killed everyone I was with. I watched a man they murdered die right in front of me. They almost killed me. I don't have your power, Kaia, and without the orb, I'm not going to be strong enough to stop them."

Kaia could feel the fear inside her sister.

"You have power," Kaia insisted. "I've felt it."

"Then you've also felt that you have more," Em replied. She sounded resentful for a moment, but then shook her head. "It's just the truth, Kaia, and I... I'm scared. When you weren't there, I didn't have the power to destroy them like you. Maybe with the orb, that would be different."

"I still don't think this is a good idea," Kaia replied. "I've felt the power of the orb, but that much power is dangerous."

"To the shadows." Em sounded determined. She obviously wanted to be as dangerous to the shadows as possible.

"And to us, too," Kaia said. "That kind of power, it burns through you. What if it's too much? What if you get hurt? Or what if we hurt other people trying to use it?"

Em shook her head. "We'd be careful."

"With that much power, there's always the temptation to use it," Kaia insisted. "And then there's the simple fact that Aunt Keris will miss the orb. She'll know it's gone, and she'll know we took it. We can't do this, Em."

"All valid points."

It wasn't her sister's voice. Kaia whirled around and saw her aunt standing at the door to the room. Kaia's eyes widened in shock, as she realized that she and her sister had been caught. She felt a sudden wash of shame and embarrassment at that. The inspector stood beside her, looking on with a disapproving gaze.

"Aunt Keris," Em began. "This isn't what it looks like."

"Of course it is, Emmeline," Aunt Keris said, stepping into the room. "You came here to take the relic. You feel that it should be yours, because it has always been twins to use it in the past. And I heard you, dear. I know how much the thought of being powerless before the shadows scares you. It scares me, too. Almost as much as the thought of losing one or both of my nieces."

Kaia heard her aunt sigh.

"But the inspector and I have been talking about what to do with it, and the honest truth is that, if we are heading into a place filled with shadows, it makes sense that the two of you should have the tool you need to fight them."

She reached into one of the folds of her dress, taking out the orb and holding it in the palm of her hand. She balanced it there, as if considering it and the power it held.

"I know that this is at least partly my fault," she said. "I misled you both. I kept things from you that I should not have. But I still feel that this is dangerous, girls. Emmeline, I heard you talking about the power the orb would give you. I understand that feeling. I know what it is like to be frightened in the face of the shadows. But it is something that could lead to more danger, for all of us. Kaia, *you* were the one talking about those dangers, and that is why I believe that you should be the one to carry the relic."

That caught Kaia by surprise. She'd been half expecting her aunt to say that neither of them was worthy now, and to hold onto the orb. Instead, she held it out to Kaia, its swirls of gold and silver seeming to shift as it got closer to her. Kaia took it, feeling the way her power flowed stronger in response to it. Em obviously felt it too, reaching out a hand for the relic. Kaia let her touch it, and the orb glowed with a light so bright it was almost blinding.

Kaia took it back, wrapping it in a scarf so that it wouldn't be too obvious as she carried it with her.

"And *both* of you will spend the rest of the trip training with me," their aunt said. "The relic is not a toy. It is a powerful weapon in the fight against the shadows."

"We'll keep it safe, Aunt Keris," Kaia promised.

"I know you will, girls. I just hope that, when we get to Athens, I am able to keep the two of *you* safe, as well."

CHAPTER FOUR

Kaia stood at the prow of the boat, looking out as Athens came into view on the horizon, feeling both a sense of trepidation at the danger that might be waiting for them all there and awe at the sight of the city ahead of her.

There were similarities to Rome in the echoes of antiquity that were on view even at this distance. Kaia could see a great ruin atop a hill at the heart of the city, pillars rising up against the sky.

"That's the Parthenon," Olivia said, moving to stand beside her, obviously seeing what Kaia was looking at. "It sits at the heart of the Acropolis, which is an ancient citadel above the city."

Those words raised Kaia's sense of dread, because the Acropolis was the spot where her aunt had told her the ritual had taken place before. Just the thought of it made Kaia's hand reach for the orb, holding it tight and feeling the way her power flared up in response to it.

"You don't have to do the ritual," Olivia said. "We don't even have to go near the Acropolis. Look, that's the spot where the Romans built a forum when they invaded, and those columns there? Those look like they might be the great temple of Zeus that once sat at the heart of the city."

Kaia was impressed that Olivia seemed to know so much about it all, but then, she'd grown up reading books about the world, taking in careful etchings that depicted places that she hadn't had a chance to go to. Kaia hadn't even had a chance to read the books. The orphanage she'd been at had assumed much more lowly futures for the girls in what passed for its care. Now, they were both there, in circumstances that no one could have foreseen.

"Thank you for trying to distract me," Kaia said with a smile. It was obvious that was what Olivia was doing, but that didn't make Kaia any less grateful for it. With every moment, the city grew closer, square, white houses mixed in with moments of brightly painted gaudiness, yet all Kaia could think about was the prospect of what might be waiting for her, for all of them, there. The shadows, and also the looming threat of the ritual, and what it would mean if she and Em performed it.

The others were getting ready to disembark as they got closer. The inspector and Aunt Keris were both waiting with their bags beside them already. Em was off to one side with Casper again. Slowly, the boat came into a harbor that looked almost as ancient as some of the ruins that rose above the city. There were fishing boats there, and pleasure boats, along with a couple that looked as if they might have belonged to the Greek navy.

The boat bumped against the dock and Kaia ran to get her things. She hurried back on deck and down a gangplank leading to the shore. As she set foot in Athens, it was almost like she could feel the history of the place around her, the past seeming to have a weight of its own.

"This is a place of myths and legends," Inspector Pinsley said. "And now, after all I have seen, I find myself wondering how many of them might be true."

"It is complex," Aunt Keris said. "We suspect that many of the old legends talk about people possessed by shadows, and those who fought them. But it's also possible that some of those legends were real, and that other things walked the earth. Not all of the magic in the world is about the shadows."

That was a strange thought. The idea that there might really have been gods and monsters walking the world was incredible, but Kaia also knew that there were still plenty of things happening in the world that she would have thought of as impossible just a few months ago.

"How do we begin with all of this?" Em asked. "Do we try to find somewhere to stay?"

That seemed like a good idea to Kaia, but to her surprise, her aunt was already shaking her head.

"I want to get to the spot where the shadowseers were killed," Aunt Keris said. "We have already taken so much time on the journey that I fear there might not be anything left to see there. I don't want to risk a moment more. Besides, I want to do this as quickly as possible. If we're lucky, we won't even have to spend the night here."

She sounded as if she wanted to get out of Athens as soon as she could, and Kaia found herself wondering if that was an attempt to protect her and Em.

"I would like to see the spot, too," Inspector Pinsley said. "But do we know exactly where it was?"

Casper cut in. "The location was in the message I picked up. It's a square in the city, with a statue of Psyche and Eros."

"We can ask around until we find it," the inspector said. "Although that might prove tricky. My Ancient Greek is passable, but my modern is not so good."

"I have a little," Aunt Keris said, sounding slightly triumphant.

And we can get everything we need, Em sent to Kaia.

She had a point. They'd done it in other places now, so many times that it was almost becoming second nature. Kaia could speak several languages now that she hadn't been able to before all of this began, the knowledge absorbed directly, along with an almost perfect understanding of the individuals around her.

They walked up to one of the dockhands, a large man with a bushy dark mustache. Em reached out for Kaia's hand, and Kaia touched it, feeling their powers rise up in response to one another, flowing through invisible channels within them, light seeming to well inside each of them.

Their power burst out, and now it enfolded the dockhand, flowing through him and forming connections like invisible strands linking him to Kaia and Em.

In that moment, Kaia understood him perfectly. She knew that he was tired from working all day. She knew that he was looking forward to getting home, to seeing his daughters again. She knew that she and Em reminded him a little of those daughters, and that he was wondering what they were doing.

Language flowed into her, and when Kaia opened her mouth next, she was speaking perfect Greek.

"Excuse me," she said. "We're looking for somewhere."

"Where's that?" the man said, sounding a little surprised that Kaia was speaking his language.

Em answered, and her Greek was as fluent as Kaia's. "A square where there's a fountain of Eros and Psyche. Our aunt says that she just *has* to see it."

She made it sound as if they were typical travelers off on the grand tour, there to take in the sights of the city, to make etchings of the antiquities and to write poems about the spaces they'd been through.

"I know the place," the dockhand said. "It's not too far. You go up that way until you reach a taverna with a blue door, then turn left. You can't miss it."

Thanking him, Kaia went back to her aunt.

"Em and I know where the fountain is."

"And it seems that you both speak Greek now," Aunt Keris observed. Kaia couldn't tell if she was impressed or worried by the ease with which they'd both done it. She gestured to the city. "Lead the way then, girls."

It felt strange to Kaia to be the one leading the way through Athens, as if she were a guide who knew the way, rather than just someone with a vague set of directions to follow. People bustled about their days on the streets around her, porters moving goods up from the docks to market, hawkers shouting out their wares. Kaia could smell food cooking; it smelled like lamb, and she could feel her stomach rumbling. One downside to not finding lodgings first was that there was no chance to eat before they set out on their investigations.

She focused on the city instead, trying to spot the taverna with the blue door. Kaia saw statues here and there lining the streets, ancient and marble, just left there as if they weren't anything special, just a normal part of life in the city.

"There," Em said, pointing.

Sure enough, there was a taverna with a blue door. Kaia turned left at it, following a much smaller street now. It led to a kind of enclosed courtyard, and that courtyard held a fountain which curved outward in a broad bowl, decorated with seashells. Statues of two figures stood entwined atop it.

"Psyche and Eros," Olivia said. "This is the place."

It had to be, and the six of them moved in, checking the square. There weren't any signs of a struggle that Kaia could see. There certainly weren't any bodies. She guessed that those would have been removed, though. What was more interesting was that there weren't any of the local police there, guarding things or looking around. Did that mean that they'd finished their work, or had they never had a chance to do it? Had someone simply covered up twelve deaths, as if they had never happened?

She watched the inspector and her aunt walking around the square together, and they might have looked like some fashionable couple out for a stroll if it weren't for the way they kept darting off to stare at things. There couldn't be much to look at, after a couple of days of people walking through the square, but they seemed to find things anyway.

"See here?" Aunt Keris said. "Flecks of blood."

"More here," the inspector said. "They have been scrubbed away by passing feet, or maybe by hand, but someone didn't get all of them."

"You're saying that someone cleaned here?" Olivia asked.

The inspector nodded. "It could just be someone trying to be helpful, if the local police are done with the crime scene, but I do not think so."

"And why not?" Casper asked. He was looking around too, but to Kaia, it seemed as if he were standing guard, looking for potential threats.

Aunt Keris answered, apparently wanting to show that she could keep up with the inspector's deductions.

"Because when we asked for directions to this place, there was no reaction. There is no sign that anyone knows that something happened here. Which means that the evidence was hidden."

"That is worrying," the inspector said, "because the blood that remains is consistent with the idea that people were killed here. See the crack in that cobble? It seems that someone struck it with great force, probably while trying to strike someone who had been knocked down there."

The two of them kept going, moving around the square.

"So our people really are all dead?" Casper asked. He sounded as if he'd been hoping it would all be some kind of grand mistake.

It certainly looked that way from where Kaia was standing. She tried to imagine what it must have been like for the shadowseers who had come here. They'd walked in here, and Kaia guessed that they must have been confident when they did it. Confident in their skills, confident that they could handle anything that was thrown at them.

The same way that Kaia and the others were confident. Her aunt and Casper would be confident in their shadowseer training. She and Em had confidence that came from their powers and the fact that they had the relic. The inspector probably had plenty of confidence in his skills as an investigator, and in the more violent skills he'd learned in the army.

Kaia found herself looking around then, checking for danger.

"Are we walking into an ambush too?" Kaia asked Inspector Pinsley.

He shook his head.

"No, I don't think so. I saw no signs of one on the way in, and there is no evidence that anyone has followed us. No, this is something more interesting."

He started to walk the perimeter of the square, looking closely. Kaia didn't know what he was looking *at,* but she could see the expression of concentration on Pinsley's face. The inspector had spotted something.

CHAPTER FIVE

Sebastian Pinsley walked the edges of the square, looking over the scraps of evidence, trying to piece together what had happened there, little by little. The more details they had, the more chance they had of working out exactly who was responsible.

Of course, they had the evidence of the message that the boy Casper had relayed to them. Pinsley found himself wondering about the boy in that moment. He had seen the way Casper had looked at Emmeline on the boat over, the way the two talked, and his automatic instinct had been to step in to prevent any scandal, the way an Englishman should. He had to remind himself in that moment that he wasn't the twins' father, and that his own daughter was there to keep an eye on them. He suspected that Olivia would handle that side of things far better than he could.

He also found himself worrying because of the danger that they were potentially walking into. The message had said that a whole team of shadowseers was missing, presumed dead, and yet he and Keris had agreed to come look into it rather than taking the girls somewhere safe. That wasn't the kind of thing that a police officer, or a father, did.

Yet, if they didn't continue the fight against the shadows, who would? Pinsley had seen the power that Kaia and her sister possessed, while Keris was sworn to the fight against such creatures. If they didn't look into this, there *was* no one else. They would be dooming whoever the shadows chose to attack next.

So Pinsley paced the square, trying to piece together exactly what had happened. Someone had tried to clear away the worst of it, but they hadn't done a thorough job. They'd left the scuff marks of booted feet, and the faintest smears of blood.

Pinsley read those the way a hunter might have read tracks in the dirt to follow an animal. He drew on his experience of war, and the aftermath of battlefields. He drew on everything that he had learned as an inspector in her majesty's constabulary. He took the scraps and turned them into understanding.

In his mind, figures moved like actors in a play, their imagined figures summoned by his deductions, their movements plotted out as precisely as he could based on the evidence.

24

"They entered, and they spread out," Pinsley said, moving around the fountain. "My guess is that they were surrounding someone at the fountain."

"If there were a single shadow, then they would try to ensure that it couldn't get away," Keris said. "The protocol if they couldn't take it by surprise would be to cut off its means of escape and try to contain it until the shadow could be expelled from the host."

Pinsley was prepared to take her word on that part of it. Keris possessed an intelligence every bit as ferocious as his own, and she knew the ways of the shadowseers far better than Pinsley did, even with the opportunities he'd had to observe her so far.

And he *did* observe her. She really was a most fascinating woman. Pinsley had felt himself growing closer to her ever since they'd met in Munich.

"This was not the work of a single opponent, though," Pinsley said. "I doubt that a single shadow-possessed individual could defeat so many at once, for one thing."

"Possible if they were civilians, but against shadowseers, no," Keris said.

It was good to have her agreement.

"In any case, the locations of the blood marks are wrong for that. They would be closer together if they were all acting against one target, rather than spread out like this."

Pinsley could see a couple of scuff marks around doorways, and the partial print of a boot on a low window.

"They waited in the surrounding buildings, and came out once the attention of the shadowseers was on the figure in the middle. Yet I do not believe that they took them completely by surprise."

"Why not?" Olivia asked from the side. His daughter, thankfully, hadn't been exposed to the kind of violence in her life that Pinsley had. She hadn't known war the way he had, or seen the violence of the London streets. Once, he might have tried to protect her even from this much, but now, he understood that she was entirely capable of dealing with whatever the world threw at her.

"Because the marks indicate fights," Pinsley said. He pointed to them. "They would be different if someone had just been killed without fighting back. More blood, but fewer footmarks, and certainly no damage to the stones the way there is in those two spots."

He pointed to them, so that the others could make them out. He wanted them to understand, and not just because talking it through aloud helped him to visualize the course of the events that had taken

25

place. The more the girls knew, the more likely they were to take the danger of all of this seriously, rather than wandering off to do their own thing, and the better the chance that they would be able to help.

There had been a point in all of this when Pinsley had tried to protect Kaia from the danger that came along with the events they'd been swept up in. She had found plenty of danger anyway, perhaps more than she might have if he'd included her. Now, he'd seen her walk into danger and come through it enough times that he knew that the best thing to do was give her all the information that he could.

"There are bullet holes in the wall here, here, and here," Pinsley said, pointing to them one by one.

The thought of shadow-possessed people armed with firearms made Pinsley uneasy. They were far too dangerous even without that additional threat. Suddenly, the weight of his former service revolver in his pocket didn't feel as comforting as it should have.

Were they shadow possessed, or simply normal people convinced to do the shadow's bidding? That was another question, and potentially an important one.

"Would the shadowseers have been able to feel possessed people coming?" Pinsley asked.

"You're wondering if one shadow hired locals to do this?" Keris replied. Again, Pinsley found himself more than impressed by her, and the way she kept up effortlessly with his deductions. "It's not that simple. Not every shadowseer is as powerful as Kaia or Emmeline. They might not have felt anything."

"And we've been close to possessed people without picking up on it," Kaia added. "It's like they hide within the bodies. I can feel a shadow when it's out in the open, but not when they possess someone."

And with shadowseers who weren't as powerful as Kaia, there might have been no way for them to feel shadows coming.

"Surely hiring local people still makes more sense than mass possession?" Olivia said. "Occam's razor. Why introduce additional shadows when one can explain it?"

Pinsley had to shake his head, though.

"If it's possible that it was more possessed people, then it is the likelier option. The marks on the ground indicate difficult fights, but also no casualties among those who came from the houses. That seems far more likely with possessed people than not."

"So multiple shadows," Keris said. Her tone made it clear just how little she liked that thought.

Pinsley didn't like it much either. The fights they'd had against shadows had been hard, and those had mostly been against small numbers of individuals, not large groups. But there was still more to be gained from the scene. He walked it slowly, counting, then re-counting. It was hard to be sure, because it was possible that someone had done a better job of cleaning some of the marks than others, but Pinsley didn't think that was likely. He had enough evidence to be confident of his conclusions.

"I believe someone may have survived this attack," he said.

He could see the surprised expressions on the others' faces. Except Keris's. She seemed to get it.

"Because of the message?" she said.

"Exactly. And I can make out eleven spots where fights took place, not twelve," he explained.

"The message?" Em asked.

"Because who sent it if everyone was dead?" Olivia said, obviously catching on.

"Exactly." Pinsley was proud of his daughter in that moment. He kept moving around the scene. "Casper, the message specifically said that people were dead? And it gave the location?"

"That's right," the shadowseer replied.

"Which means that it had to be someone who was here," Pinsley explained. "I briefly thought that it might be a witness, but they wouldn't understand what they saw. I also considered the possibility that it might have been a way to lure us into a trap, but that trap would have been sprung by now."

"I'm fairly sure, Father, that the way to test if something is a trap is *not* to walk straight into that trap," Olivia said, with a slight note of reproach.

And if Pinsley had worked it out beforehand, he would have insisted that the others hang back. For now, though, all he could do was keep walking the scene, trying to understand it.

"So, there might be one of the shadowseers still alive?" Emmeline said.

"I think it is very likely," Pinsley replied. He walked toward the opening to the square, on the basis that it seemed like the most likely point of exit. The possessed people would have shut the doors they entered the square by behind them.

"You think he ran this way?" Keris said.

"I think he must have. The shadows wouldn't have left a way for him to get into one of the buildings. He would have been running quickly, grabbing for anything that might let him slow his pursuers down."

Pinsley could see a mark on the floor where fruit had been spilled, too much of it to be an accident. It was only a small indication, but it was enough to keep him on the track of the escaping shadowseer.

He could see the others following close behind, but he knew he needed to focus. Pinsley had pursued people across London in the course of his career, and he'd also had to flee several times now. He understood how people ran: the initial burst of speed, the sudden twists and turns after that, then the attempt to break contact and hide.

He kept going, and reached the taverna that they'd passed on the way there. Pinsley paused outside it, staring at one of the windows on the ground floor. Its shutters were open, but one of them was damaged, as if someone had passed through that window at speed, catching the shutter on the way through.

Pinsley walked around to the door, heading inside, wanting to check. There were a few patrons there, but Pinsley's attention was on the barkeep. He went up to the man, searching for the phrases he needed in Greek.

"Did you have some trouble here recently? A man who just burst in, probably followed by people?"

The barkeep looked at him a little strangely. "How'd you know about that? Who are you, and why are you in here asking questions?"

"The man who was running is a friend of ours," Keris said. "We haven't seen him since. Do you know what happened to him?"

The barkeep shrugged. "He ran in, he ran out. Left my window broken, too."

"Which way did he run out?" Pinsley asked.

The barkeep shrugged, as if strange men running into his establishment weren't any of his business, and then pointed. "He went that way, I think."

He didn't sound confident about it, but it was all Pinsley had to go on. He left in the direction the barkeep had pointed, trying to follow down the street.

That was when he lost the trail. Simply lost it, the street too busy, any traces rubbed clean by too many feet passing that way.

"There's nothing here," Pinsley said. "I can't find any more signs. He might have come this way, but at this point, he would have been taking turnings randomly."

And without any more footprints or blood specks, Pinsley couldn't tell which turnings those were. If this had been back in London, maybe

28

he could have used his local knowledge to guess which ones, or just gone to some of his old contacts to try to find out if anyone had seen him. Here, though, in a strange city, he didn't have those options. A sense of disappointment filled him as he understood that the search was over.

"We've lost him," Pinsley said. "I'm sorry. We need to find another way to locate him."

CHAPTER SIX

Frederick Aloysius Penfold Illingworth had to admit that, the more he learned of Sebastian Pinsley and his companions, the more impressed and worried he became about the whole situation. They were clearly very dangerous individuals indeed. At the same time, he became more convinced by the moment that stopping the former inspector of the London constabulary was necessary, whatever the means.

Not that he would have done anything else anyway. Once he had been contracted to undertake something, he didn't stop. He didn't hesitate. His organization's reputation for pragmatism and determination was hard earned, and Illingworth wasn't about to ruin that reputation now.

He was a short, squat man, broad shouldered and heavyset, with features that might generously be described as froglike. His eyes were too large and his features too squashed. He had no pretensions of handsomeness or charisma, at least in the conventional sense. He had never needed either, when he had a mind as incisive as a scalpel with which to do his work. Currently, he was wearing a summer weight linen suit, its pockets filled with essentials, wearing a broad-brimmed hat to keep off the sun, and carrying his sharp-pointed umbrella by his side in case it should prove necessary later. It was better to be prepared for all eventualities, even when it came to the weather.

He was in Rome at the moment, talking to a couple of papal guards, trying to get a full sense of the impact that his quarry had had on the city.

"So," he said in flawless, unaccented Italian. "Tell me again about the ones who came here."

"There's not much to tell," one of the guards said. "A group of strange English people came here and caused chaos. For a time, we even thought that they were involved in the death of a priest, but then we were told they were *investigating* that death, instead."

"Of course they were," Mr. Illingworth said. It had never occurred to him that they might be doing anything else. Superintendent Hutton, back in London, had insisted that his inspector was a rogue who did as he pleased and was caught up in criminal endeavors. To Illingworth, it was just more evidence that the superintendent was an idiot. He found that most people were.

Everything he had found out about Pinsley before leaving London suggested that the man was brilliant, diligent, and incapable of stepping back from a mystery. His association with the young woman, Kaia, was harder to explain, but Illingworth doubted that it was as simple as the old story of an older man having his head turned and eloping, whatever more foolish people like the superintendent thought.

No, there was something more going on here, and the fact that Mr. Illingworth didn't understand quite what that something else was only made it more interesting. He would have to ask the inspector about it all when he found him.

"They caused chaos while they were here," one of the papal guards said. "Fighting in the streets, desecrating sacred sites, wandering the catacombs at random."

Illingworth doubted that there had been anything random about it all. People like Pinsley didn't make random decisions. They acted with a purpose. It was simply a matter of comprehending what that purpose might be. He plotted every piece of new information onto the mental map he was building of it all, trying to establish what had happened, and where his quarry had gone.

That was the part that mattered. The *only* part that mattered.

People had called Illingworth cruel in the past, even loathsome. It only showed their lack of understanding. Mr. Illingworth achieved the things he was being paid to achieve, whether that was bringing down a government minister, helping to establish a trading route, or capturing a wanted fugitive.

It was simply that he was prepared to use whatever means he needed to in order to achieve those ends, unencumbered by concerns of morality that might hold back a lesser mind.

His understanding was that Inspector Pinsley *did* abide by such strictures. It was surprising, and a little disappointing. This man was supposed to be his equal, but how could he be when he was so... limited? Still, a man like Mr. Illingworth didn't get to where he was today by hoping for contests against true equals. A near equal was far better, with a hard fight, followed by a swift victory.

"Do you know what happened to them when you let them go?" Illingworth asked the papal guards.

The one who'd been speaking shrugged. "Last I heard, they left the city."

"Going where?"

That just got another shrug.

"Once they're out of the city, who cares?"

Illingworth held back his frustration at the lack of an answer. It was too much to hope that the kind of fools employed as guards in a place like this would have thought to watch which way visitors left in case someone needed to follow.

In any case, there were… other places he could ask.

*

Illingworth waited at a small café on the edge of the city. He'd sent a message by cable several hours ago, and picked up a packet of coded answers in return. To kill time while he waited, he took out his thick leather notebook and a fountain pen, updating his notes in his own carefully crafted cipher. One no mind other than his could hope to crack.

Those notes were a big part of the reason why he was able to operate so effectively. He had people gathering information, picking up fragments that Illingworth's mind pieced together into more. His little notebook had information that could probably topple governments, if he chose, along with numbers for several discreet accounts, and details for some of his more useful agents.

It was two much *less* useful ones Illingworth was waiting for now. Two who had failed before, while spinning a most unbelievable story.

They approached now, Jones and Hale, the former large and powerfully built, dressed in a long coachman's jacket that usually hid a variety of weapons, the latter wiry and dangerous, his shirt sleeves rolled up, a flat cap covering his head. Two of his most reliable bounty hunters, or at least so he'd thought, until they'd failed to bring in the inspector.

They came forward now, almost nervously, considering what large men they were, used to violence. Good, it meant that they understood just how badly they'd failed.

"Gentlemen," Illingworth said, standing. "I have come here personally because I intend to do what you could not."

"You're going after Pinsley and the freaks he's traveling with?" Hale asked. He sounded surprised, when Illingworth didn't feel that he had any reason to do so.

"When we accept a job, gentlemen, we do not give up on that, do we?"

They both looked slightly sheepish at that, which was amusing, considering the size of the two and the skills they had in violence.

"Um…" Jones said. "That wasn't our fault. The girl with them… she did something. Something impossible. She sent us both flying with a wave of her hand."

Illingworth made a small sound of irritation. "If you are going to lie to me, at least make it vaguely believable."

"It's the truth!" Hale said. The strange thing was that he looked as though he believed it, and Illingworth was normally very good at spotting a liar.

"You want me to believe that some girl used… what? Magical powers to defeat you?" Illingworth scoffed. He was nothing if not a man of reason. Superstitious beliefs could be useful, but only in so far as they allowed a man like him to achieve what he wanted to achieve. He certainly wasn't about to believe that two tough, strong men had been brought low by the efforts of one girl.

No, something else had happened, something else that embarrassed them or that they wanted to hold back from telling him. Perhaps they had been taken by surprise, or perhaps they had simply accepted a bribe. Either way, the result was the same: they had failed.

"Do you have any information for me on which way the subjects went after they left Rome?" Illingworth asked.

"We kept an eye on the local ports," Jones said. "We believe that they may have headed in the direction of Athens."

"May?" Illingworth was really struggling to keep his patience at this point. "You didn't think to confirm it?"

"Didn't want to get too close," Jones said.

"In case the magical girl got to you again?" Illingworth asked.

Jones gave him a surprisingly direct look. A look that held fear, or at least the memory of it. "Yes."

Illingworth found himself tiring of this nonsense. If these men couldn't help him, then he was wasting his time by even talking to them.

"That will be all, I think," Illingworth said, taking his notebook and putting it away in his pocket. "Do I need to say that your services will no longer be required by my organization?"

"No longer… you're *firing* us?" Jones said. "You haven't even *paid* us for this job."

"Paid you?" Illingworth said. He rested his hand lightly on his umbrella, holding it the way a dandy might have held a cane. "Why would I pay you for a job that you haven't completed?"

"Now listen—" Jones said, reaching out to grab for Illingworth.

That was a mistake. Illingworth took hold of his wrist as he reached, twisting it painfully, then hooked his umbrella behind the other man's leg, sending him sprawling to the ground.

He was ready for the moment when Hale ran in, trying to protect his compatriot. Illingworth stepped to the side, jabbing the point of the umbrella through the big man's thigh. He cried out, stumbling.

Jones was back on his feet then, throwing a punch toward Illingworth's head. He ducked, letting the wild swing pass over him, then whipped the umbrella around in a two-handed blow that brought the handle crashing into the other man's jaw. He hit the ground hard.

Illingworth saw both men start to reach into pockets, but he was faster, drawing out a small, squat revolver.

"Do either of you believe that I will have the slightest compunction about killing you?" Illingworth asked. "After you've failed? After you've threatened me? Only the possibility of complications with the local authorities is preventing me from doing it right now."

Honestly, with men like this, it might be easier to kill them, yet doing so would raise unnecessary difficulties and slow Illingworth down. Besides, the two had come up with one usable fragment of information.

Athens.

Illingworth walked off, checking the wires he had received with small fragments of information. There was a note there that caught his attention, a small fragment of news, an interception. It seemed that twelve people were missing in Athens, members of one of the many small secret societies the world possessed.

It was a mystery. Exactly the kind of mystery that Illingworth suspected Inspector Pinsley might relish.

Combine that with the fragment his operatives had given him, along with the simple path of the fugitive's journey so far, and it seemed probable that Inspector Pinsley was somewhere in Athens.

Mr. Illingworth had a boat to catch.

*

Illingworth stared out over the water, waiting for the capital of Greece to come into sight. He checked his small stash of weapons as he did so. His umbrella, of course. His revolver. A knife he kept inside his jacket in case of emergencies. He had a pair of cuffs to hold his captive, and letters stating his authority. He hadn't even had to forge most of them. It was more than sufficient to do the job.

The only question now was what kind of opposition he might face. He didn't believe this nonsense about magic, but there seemed to be no doubt that the inspector had some kind of support with him. The young woman? His daughter? Perhaps the other woman who was traveling with him? From what Illingworth understood from his research, she certainly seemed to represent a threat beyond those that women normally did.

Ultimately, it didn't matter. It didn't matter that he'd had to travel across the length of Europe to do this. It didn't matter that the inspector had people with him. It didn't even matter that he considered his client to be an incompetent, and the reasons for his request to be as much about petty jealousy as anything.

All that mattered was the job. However Pinsley had escaped Mr. Illingworth's men, the fact was that it had damaged his reputation, and that of his organization. That was unacceptable. Illingworth had to make this right, had to capture Pinsley, had to bring him back to face whatever passed for justice in London.

That was his task, and so that was what would happen. It didn't matter that the inspector was intelligent; Illingworth was more intelligent. It didn't matter that he had help, because Illingworth had every advantage he needed. He was stronger, more ruthless, and was not going to give up.

He would bring Sebastian Pinsley back, dead or alive.

CHAPTER SEVEN

Kaia could see the inspector's disappointment that they hadn't been able to find the shadowseer who had escaped the ambush. He obviously thought that he should be able to follow the trail all the way back to wherever the man was hiding, while Kaia was pretty impressed that he'd managed to lead them all even as far as he had.

"The question is how we locate the missing shadowseer now," Aunt Keris said.

"We could ask around to see if anyone has seen him," Em suggested.

The inspector shook his head. "I doubt that will work if this individual believes that they are being hunted by the shadows. I assume that they will take countermeasures?"

He looked over to Aunt Keris as he asked that.

She nodded. "We shadowseers are trained to stay out of sight. The shadows try to target us, even as we attempt to drive them out, and there is always the possibility of an angry mob arriving at our doors if ordinary people see us doing something that they cannot explain. If we were not good at hiding, there would be none of us left."

Which meant that it might be difficult to find the missing shadowseer that way.

"There might still be traces," Casper suggested. "The right question in the right place might find him for us."

"Even if that is true, it will take time," the inspector said. He looked up pointedly to the sky. It was starting to darken, gradually heading toward dusk. "And we cannot spend all night trying to find him, when we have no idea if we will actually catch up to him or not."

"And if there *are* clues out there, you can bet that the shadows are trying to follow them," Aunt Keris said. "No, we need something more direct. We need to work out where they might go, rather than trying to follow them step by step."

"Would there be a safehouse in the city, the way there was in Munich?" Olivia asked.

It seemed like a good question to Kaia. If there was such a safehouse, then it made sense that a shadowseer who had been attacked would run back there, trying to get to somewhere safe. Kaia suspected

36

that if she had found herself in danger in London, she might try to get back to the church where she had a room in the rectory, while if she were in Munich, she might well try to reach the safehouse where she had met her aunt.

"There would," Aunt Keris said. "The problem is that I do not have its location. The people from one safehouse are not given locations for others, in case they are compromised or captured."

Kaia guessed that was sensible, when the shadows could potentially take over anyone, and pick out memories once they were in someone's head. Yes, shadowseers had defenses against such things, but those defenses could be broken down if they were hurt enough, or drugged, or simply tortured to the point where they couldn't keep the shadows out.

Kaia swallowed as she realized just how much her life had changed, to the point that she could think about things like that.

"So we cannot find them?" Olivia asked.

"Maybe," her father replied. "Given time, I should be able to work out enough of how Athens works to locate the one who escaped."

"And we will be able to use some of our methods of communication to locate the safehouse," Aunt Keris said. "Again, though, that will take time, and we may not *have* time. For all we know, the shadowseer is badly wounded, even dying. At the very least, the shadows or their agents will still be hunting them. We need to get to them first."

Kaia could hear her aunt's frustration. She wanted to be able to help. She wanted to find the shadowseer and give them all a chance to get to them before the shadows did.

Then she realized that she might actually have a chance to do that.

"I think we might be able to find the shadowseer," Kaia said to Em. "Think about when we've seen things before. Think about how we can feel the power in other shadowseers."

Her twin looked thoughtful for a moment or two. "It's possible. But over an entire city?"

"I bet we can do it between us," Kaia said. "We have to at least try."

She held out her hand, holding the orb there because Kaia hoped that it would provide an extra boost to their power.

She felt that power rise up as Em's hand closed over hers with the relic between them, rising up from a deep well within her. Those powers entwined until Kaia couldn't tell whose was whose, building up until the pressure of it felt as though it might burst inside Kaia's skull.

The power flowed out from Kaia in a wave, and as it did so, she *saw*.

Athens was spread out beneath her then, the streets and houses down below her like a map. Kaia could feel Em there with her, able to see all that she could see, feel all that she could feel.

Kaia felt a moment of fear as she realized that she could make out the presence of shadows there, easily as many as they had encountered in Rome. The city seemed to teem with them, so that she could sense them almost in every corner.

Then there was the Acropolis. It seemed to pulse with dormant power, lines of it flickering around the Parthenon, something about those lines drawing Kaia in. It pulled Kaia forward, and she herself drifting toward it, staring at it, feeling the pressure of it, feeling the power there…

Kaia, wait, Em sent to her. *Don't get drawn in!*

Kaia felt the pull of the place then, felt the power there of the ritual site, and it was hard to pull back from it.

Kaia!

The force of Em's thoughts allowed Kaia to snap her eyes away from the Acropolis. She realized how close she'd come to getting caught up in the power there. Without her sister, would she have gone into the middle of it? What would have happened then?

Kaia didn't want to know. She wanted to focus on finding the shadowseer. She concentrated, reaching out across the city for the same signature of power that she felt in Em, or her aunt, or Casper.

It was there, the faintest whisper, and Kaia felt herself drifting toward it, trying to be sure of the location. She tried to focus on the direction, and on the flowing plan of the streets below her. She drifted closer and saw a house, blue painted, with marble busts set around the edge of the roof like guardians.

She and Em flowed through the walls of that house smoothly. Kaia saw a young man there with dark hair, wrapping bandages around a wound to his side. Kaia wanted to communicate with him, wanted to find a way to tell him that they were coming, and that they were on his side.

There was no way to do it, though, and already, Kaia could feel the vision fading…

She came back to herself with a gasp as she took in air, blinking in the fading light as her mind grew accustomed to being back in her body. Em was still there, just a pace or two away, and Kaia could see her making the same adjustment.

"We know where the shadowseer is," Em said.

"What?" Aunt Keris said.

"We saw him," Kaia explained. "This way."

She and Em started to lead the way through the city, its history and beauty less important now than simply trying to remember the way through its streets. Kaia had seen where the house was, and she had felt the pulse of the shadowseer's presence, but now that they were back in their bodies, it was more difficult.

They'd seen the city from above like a map, but now they were back at ground level, trying to work out which streets correlated to the ones they'd seen from above. Em seemed confident, striding forward as if it were impossible that she could ever truly be lost.

The others followed in Kaia and Em's wake, hurrying along because Em was moving quickly and Kaia was keeping pace with her. Already, Kaia could feel the details of the things she'd seen starting to fade. She felt as though she and Em needed to hurry just so that they would be able to remember the way.

"This way," Em said, taking a turning. Kaia followed her, starting to worry now about the time that it was taking to get there. Were they going the wrong way? Had they taken a wrong turn somewhere so that they would find themselves wandering the city trying to find the right place for hours?

No, this was the right street, because Kaia could see the house ahead there, the same one that she'd seen, with the same marble busts set around its edges, of what Kaia assumed were figures from Greek myths.

"There," Em said, obviously recognizing it too. She led the way up to the front door before the others could stop her.

Casper was there then with her, working on the lock with a small set of picks. In just moments, it sprang open.

"Let me go first," he said. "It might not be—"

But Em was already moving past him into the house, and Kaia knew that she had to go with her sister, or risk Em wandering into danger alone. Even as the inspector, her aunt, and Olivia followed them into the house, Kaia and Em were already making their way up a staircase.

They could feel the shadowseer's presence again now, in some echo of the feeling they'd had from the vision. The house was large and empty seeming, with pictures on the walls that might have been images from myths or might have been depictions of shadowseers about their work; certainly, one seemed to show a shadow being driven out of a monstrous wolf, the darkness flowing out in the face of light being poured into it. It reminded Kaia far too closely of the things she'd done in the past.

The two of them ran up the stairs, reaching a landing where a partially open door stood at the end. Kaia saw Em push it open. A young man was there, wearing dark trousers and a loose shirt, sitting on the edge of a broad bed across from a window whose open shutters let in the evening air.

Kaia saw that young man look up in obvious fear, and then he ran for the window.

"Wait!" Kaia called out, but he was already diving out of it, onto a flat rooftop beyond.

She saw Em run after him without hesitation, throwing herself through just a step behind. Kaia cursed to herself and set off after her sister with all the speed she could muster. She clambered through the window and found herself on an open rooftop. The young man was almost at the edge of it already, leaping across a short gap to another roof.

Em leapt after him, and Kaia forced herself to jump after her. She landed on the next roof, continuing to run, trying to keep up as her sister and the shadowseer ran on. They made another leap, this one wider, and this time, Kaia had to throw herself at it, grabbing the far edge with her hands and pulling herself up.

This roof was broad and flat, with a staircase leading down one side to street level.

Neither Em nor the shadowseer went for the stairs; instead, the shadowseer reached the far end of the roof and just... dropped.

Em followed him to the edge, looked down for a moment, and then jumped down after him.

Em, no! Kaia sent, running to the edge of the roof, barely able to bring herself to look down.

There was an awning below, damaged now by the impact of two people jumping down onto it to get to street level, but it was obviously how Em and the shadowseer had survived the fall. Kaia couldn't jump down the same way, so she ran around to the stairs instead, heading down them even as Aunt Keris and the inspector made it over onto the roof.

Kaia didn't slow down. She had to get to her sister. If the shadowseer thought that Em was a threat, he might lash out without thinking, might hurt or even kill her. Kaia had to get to her sister before it came to that.

She ran down the stairs and sprinted for the corner of the building, hoping that she could catch up to her sister before it came to any kind of violence.

Hold on, Em, I'm coming, she sent.

She kept running, skidding around the edge of the building. There she found Em struggling with a young man, who was lashing out with fists and feet, Em barely avoiding them. Kaia had the feeling that he was hurt or tired, because he was moving slowly, and when she looked closer, she could see dried blood on his clothes.

Kaia rushed forward, and as she did so, the young man's head snapped around toward her. Em, seeing her chance, stepped in and swept his feet out from under him in a move that their aunt had taught them both.

Kaia summoned her power then, the glow of it filling her.

"Stop!" she said to the young man. "We aren't shadows. We're here to help."

Aunt Keris, the inspector, Olivia, and Casper all came hurrying up in Kaia's wake. They all looked ready for the possibility of violence too.

The young shadowseer sat staring up at Kaia.

"As soon as the lady got close," the shadowseer said in Greek, "I could feel that she was like me. You are all shadowseers?"

"We are," Aunt Keris said, apparently deciding that it was better to gloss over the part where half of them weren't. "And we need to talk to you about what happened to your group. But first, we should get off the street. It isn't safe out here."

CHAPTER EIGHT

Kaia sat in the safehouse, waiting for the shadowseer they'd found, Nasos, to explain exactly what was going on.

They were all in what appeared to be a dining room, seated around a large, rustic wooden table. Olivia had gone into a small kitchen there and come out with a selection of cooked meats, olives, and bread, which Kaia dug into hungrily. She hadn't realized quite how long it had been since she last ate.

"We'll stay here while we're in the city," Aunt Kaia declared. "We will be safer here than anywhere else. Now, Nasos?"

"Yes?" There was a note of respect there. Kaia had the feeling that he knew who her aunt was, even if it was clear that the two of them had never met one another before.

"We need you to tell us all what happened to you, and to your group."

Kaia caught the look of pain that crossed Nasos's face. He couldn't be much more than her age, dark haired and dark eyed. He looked haunted, as if he had seen too much.

"Our group stays in the city," he said. "It is our job to look after the ritual site, to make sure that there are no shadows here, so that if it is ever needed then it will be safe to use it."

"Safe," Em muttered, in a doubtful tone.

Shh, Em, I'm listening, Kaia sent to her.

I'm just saying that it's only safe *for the people who aren't doing the ritual. Not for* us.

No, it wouldn't be safe. Their aunt had been perfectly clear about that. More than that, Kaia had felt the dangerous power in the Acropolis for herself, when she had almost been pulled into it as she looked out over the city.

"We protect the site," Nasos said. "Some of us go out from time to time to work with other groups, so that we can do our part against the shadows, but mostly we just stay here and train, ready to deal with any shadows that make it into the city."

"Does that happen often?" Olivia asked. "Do you have to fight many shadows?"

"They come through occasionally," Nasos said. "But not as often as in other places, because they know that there is a whole group of shadowseers in the city watching for them. There hadn't been any for months. We thought that they had learned to stay away from Athens."

"But they hadn't," the inspector said. "Did you notice the moment when more came into the city?"

"We thought that there was one," Nasos said. "We could sense it, and for all of us to sense it so clearly... I'm not strong, not like some are, not like *you* are." He looked in Kaia and Em's direction. "But I could still feel it. We knew that it had to be powerful."

That caught Kaia's interest. She'd felt a host of different shadows back in Rome. Some had felt more powerful, more dangerous, than others. One that the shadowseers could feel across the city... well, Kaia didn't know how strong that would be, because she and Em had been able to feel all of them. If what Nasos was saying was true, though, it suggested that there was at least one out there with considerable power.

"It was powerful," Aunt Keris said, "but it was also drawing you in?"

"We didn't know that at the time," Nasos replied. "We thought... it led us on a chase around the city, so that we had to track it down, triangulating its position by what we could feel. Finally, we thought we had it cornered. We thought it was trapped, but *we* were the ones who were trapped."

Now, Kaia could see the pain in his expression, as if just remembering this moment hurt him.

"We went in there, and the shadow was just smiling. It had taken the body of a young woman, and she didn't seem bothered by the fact that a dozen shadowseers were spreading out around her. I tried to tell the others that there was something wrong, but they didn't listen."

"Was that when additional possessed individuals came out of the surrounding buildings?" Inspector Pinsley asked.

Kaia caught Nasos's look of surprise. Evidently, so did the inspector.

"I looked over the scene," he said. "It was the only logical interpretation of the evidence."

Kaia saw Nasos nod.

"They were all around us," he said. "I wanted to stay and fight, but Andreas said that someone had to get the word out. So I ran. I ran as fast as I could, but even then one of them cut me. I barely got out of there, and it took everything I had to lose them. Then I cabled a message out to warn everyone else."

"It sounds like a very close call," Aunt Keris said, in a sympathetic tone. "Tell me, Nasos, do you have any idea what so many shadows are doing here? Do you think it was just to wipe out your group?"

"That wouldn't be enough for them?" Casper asked, but Aunt Keris was already shaking her head.

"They will take us on and target us, but generally only if it brings them closer to some goal. We are threats to them because we stand between them and their ends. In this case, luring a whole cadre of our kind into a trap suggests that something else is going on."

"They're planning something," Nasos agreed. "They taunted us with it before they started killing us, but they wouldn't say what."

"A portal, maybe?" Kaia suggested. Kaia thought about the portals that she'd seen in Paris and in Rome. They'd been stone arches, worked with runes that had focused the power needed to hold them open. In Paris, that power had been due to come from the sacrifice of one of their number, but Kaia and the inspector had stopped it from happening. In Rome, the portal had already been open, letting Kaia look through into the shadows' realm.

It had been like looking into an endless sea of night.

"It fits with what they've done before," the inspector agreed. "Although the question is when."

"If they're doing it here," Aunt Keris said, "there must be a reason for it. There must be a reason why they want to be so close to the ritual site…"

She seemed to think for a moment or two, and then snapped her fingers as something came to her.

"Nasos, did your patrols in the city usually peak around any particular time?"

"At the full moon," Nasos said. "Why?"

Aunt Keris looked as if she'd just confirmed something she was thinking.

"What is it?" Kaia asked.

"The power of the ritual site is not a constant," Aunt Keris said. "Its powers flow from the cycles of the world. The legends talk about the first ritual taking place at a time of great power. The full moon would be just such a time."

"That's tomorrow night," the inspector said. Apparently, the phases of the moon were just another strand of information that he had tucked away in his memory.

"So, shadows are planning to open a portal tomorrow," Aunt Keris said. "Using the ritual site, that portal could be huge."

Yet that wasn't the worst part. That wasn't the part that filled Kaia with the greatest fear.

Em had obviously caught it too.

"And this will take place at the Acropolis?" her sister said. Em didn't look happy. "Kaia, we can't go there. We said that we wouldn't go there."

"I know," Kaia said. She didn't like it any more than her sister did. "But we may not have a choice. Not if they're going to do something like this."

Nasos frowned at them. "I don't understand. What are you... wait, you're twins. Like in the legends."

"No," Em said. "*Not* like in the legends. Because all of those tried to do your stupid ritual, and they died. And *we're* not going to do it."

Aunt Keris cut in then. "No one is making you perform the ritual, Emmeline."

Em didn't look convinced. "Really? Because when we were on the boat, you were telling me that we wouldn't have to go anywhere near the Acropolis, but here we are."

"What would you have me do?" Aunt Keris asked. "Stand by and let shadows overrun the world?"

That was the problem. Kaia couldn't stand back while something like that happened. She couldn't just hold off for the sake of her own safety if it meant that shadows would just pour into the world. That wouldn't be right. She wouldn't be able to live with herself if that happened.

"We have to at least try to stop them, Em," Kaia said. "We don't have to do the ritual, but if we get close enough, I might be able to close the portal."

"*Why* do we have to try?" Em said. "Because it's our destiny? Because we're some kind of chosen ones who have to give up our lives to save the rest of the world? Nobody *asked* me if I wanted to be their fated hero, Kaia."

"Nobody asked me either," Kaia said. "But this isn't about fate, or destiny, or anything like that."

"Then what *is* it about?" Em asked. "What's one more portal? It's not like the shadows can take over anyone who isn't corrupt, or mad."

Kaia was pretty sure that her sister knew the answer anyway. She got that Em was scared, but she had to see how this worked.

"It's about the fact that we *can* do something," Kaia said. "If we have the power to help people and we don't, then that's a choice. We

45

can't just say that it has nothing to do with us. We would have everything the shadows did on us."

"Then there's the fact that the shadows would hardly leave us alone once they came through the portal," Aunt Keris said. "We would still have to fight them, only having already missed our best chance to stop them."

"I still don't like this," Em said. "I don't want to die playing the part of some stupid *hero*, Kaia, and I don't want you to die either. Not when we've only just found one another. Not when there's still so much I want to do."

Was it Kaia's imagination, or did her eyes dart over to Casper as she said that?

"Emmeline," Aunt Keris said. "I must insist—"

"You don't get to tell me what I do and when I risk my life!" Em snapped back.

"You are a shadowseer!" Nasos said, joining in. "I saw all the protectors of Athens killed, and you have the power to stop the shadows who did it. You have a duty!"

"I don't have a duty to die for anyone," Em said, and stormed out.

CHAPTER NINE

Kaia was walking through a set of ruins searching for something, but she couldn't remember what, or why. Great columns rose up on every side of her like a forest of stone, blocking her view, making it impossible to know for sure which way she was going.

Still she pushed forward, knowing that she was there for a reason, that there was something, some*one* that she had to find, and that it mattered more than anything else in the world.

Kaia was alone as she wandered the ruins, wearing a long white dress and sandals, like something out of one of the paintings of Greek myth she'd seen. The sun beat down on her, throwing the shadows of the columns at odd angles that meant she had to take strange paths through the stone forest to avoid stepping in them.

It was important not to step in them, even if Kaia couldn't remember exactly why. She kept moving through the columns, kept picking her way around the shadows. Then, ahead, she saw him: tall, in his forties, with a lean face Kaia would never be able to forget.

The inspector. She was searching for the inspector.

"Inspector!" Kaia called out, and Inspector Pinsley waved back at her, but then he set off among the columns, so that Kaia had to hurry to keep up, almost dancing her way among the shadows at the bases of the columns now.

Only those shadows weren't staying still. They were reaching out for Kaia with tendrils of darkness, so that Kaia had to dodge and weave to avoid them, continuing to move forward, trying to catch up to Pinsley as he hurried on through the ruins.

She saw him ahead now, approaching an open space among the columns. There was a kind of raised dais there, and the shadows of the surrounding columns fell on it, forming an X.

Even as Kaia watched in horror, the inspector stepped right into the heart of that X.

Shadows wrapped around him, pulling him, down as if the floor were made of quicksand. Kaia rushed over, trying to help him, wanting to pull him free, but he sank so quickly that Kaia couldn't reach him in time, not skipping among the shadows as she was.

47

She saw the inspector vanish, and her horror at the sight of that called up her power, light bursting out around her, flaring so brightly that it burned the shadows away, so brightly that it burned her eye, so brightly that...

Kaia woke to sun streaming through the window, the remnants of the nightmare making her sit bolt upright. Her sister was awake on a bed across from her in the room they were sharing in the safehouse, and she was staring at Kaia.

"Kaia, you're glowing."

Kaia held a hand up to look at and realized that Em was right. The glow of her power surrounded her like a golden aura. It must have flared up in response to her nightmare.

Kaia pushed it back down, telling herself that it was *just* a nightmare, and that there was nothing to worry about. Yet, where her powers were concerned, was anything ever so simple?

"I think I need to check on the inspector," she said. She wanted to see him, to be sure that he was all right.

She got up and dressed as quickly as she could in a simple cream and blue traveling dress. Em also got up, dressing in a slightly darker dress set with small red lace bows.

"I'll come with you," she said. "But I doubt there's anything you need to worry about. About the worst thing we might find is him coming out of Aunt Keris's room."

The two of them had been getting pretty close recently. Kaia had seen how alone and how grief filled the inspector had been when she'd first met him, while her aunt seemed to carry the weight of the world on her shoulders, treating the whole fight against the shadows as if it were solely her responsibility. If the two of them found some happiness, maybe that was a good thing.

For now, though, she wanted to make sure that the inspector was all right. Kaia hurried downstairs, went through to the dining room, and froze in place, because what she saw there was too awful to do anything else.

Nasos sat at the dining table, in the same spot he'd been in last night. Only now he was slumped against the chair, his head lolling at an obscene angle. A red gash ran all the way across his throat where someone had cut it, and blood stained the wood of the floor all around.

Kaia cried out at the horror of it all without meaning to. Em pushed forward as she did so.

"What is it, Kaia, what's... oh, no. Help! Everyone help!"

48

She called it out loud enough to wake everyone in the house. It was what Kaia knew she should have done, but she still couldn't stop herself staring at Nasos's dead form, just sitting there, obviously taken by surprise and killed before he could even react. How could someone do such a thing? *Who* had done it? Even after having seen so many murders, Kaia still found herself reacting to the sight of the dead young shadowseer.

Kaia heard the sound of running footsteps behind her, and she turned to see Aunt Keris hurrying down the stairs, a long knife and a club in her hands, ready to fight. Casper was just a pace or two behind her, a length of chain wrapped around his knuckles. Kaia realized that when Em had called for help, they must have thought that the safehouse was under attack.

Even Olivia came running down the stairs, looking worried. Kaia was surprised to see that she had found a heavy walking stick from somewhere, obviously determined to do her part in any fight.

Kaia saw the moment when they all spotted Nasos's body, because the three of them came to a sudden halt, simply staring. Kaia could see the horror on Olivia's face, the worry on Aunt Keris's and the sudden wariness in Casper.

"What happened here?" Aunt Keris asked.

"We don't know," Kaia said. "We came downstairs and just found him like this."

"*Exactly* like this?" Aunt Keris asked. It was clear that the details mattered. Kaia had seen how the inspector went about looking over a crime scene, and it seemed that her aunt was doing the same thing.

"We haven't touched anything," Em said. "We haven't even gone into the room. We only just got here."

"The killer could still be in the house," Casper pointed out.

That thought made Kaia's blood run cold. Were they in there with a killer? Were they about to be attacked the way Nasos had been?

Her aunt took a moment to look over the room, and then took charge.

"The blood is fresh enough that you could be right. Casper, I want you to secure the house. Olivia, I need you to go and wake your father up. Be careful, both of you, and shout if you see anything out of the ordinary."

They both ran off to undertake the tasks Aunt Keris had set for them. Meanwhile, Kaia found herself moving forward with her aunt as she went into the room, looking over the scene of the murder.

It was horrible being so close to something like that. It didn't get easier just because Kaia had been close to bodies before. This was someone she had been talking to just last night. Someone who had already survived one attack by the shadows, only to be cut down now.

"This was the shadows, wasn't it?" Em asked. "The ones who killed the others?"

"It looks that way," Aunt Keris said. "They are the most logical ones to try to target Nasos here, especially since they are planning to open that portal of theirs. They would want to take out the last potential opposition to that."

"What about us?" Em asked. "If they were trying to kill anyone who could stop them, why not kill us?"

"I don't know," their aunt admitted. "Perhaps they did not realize that we were here. Perhaps they were scared off before they could do anything else, or perhaps there is some other reason."

Even as she spoke, Casper came back in. "The house appears to be secure. I can't find any sign of an attacker within it, although the front door is unlocked."

Suggesting that the killer had come in and left that way. Kaia tried to imagine someone brazen enough to enter the house so openly, but if this was the work of someone possessed by a shadow, then they wouldn't care. They would do what they were forced to do. More than that, Kaia had seen people possessed by shadows who could bend light around them, weaving the shadows so that they were harder for normal people to see. In a doorway, working on a lock, they wouldn't have to worry about anyone spotting them at all.

Kaia was still considering the implications of that when Olivia came down the stairs. Kaia could see the concern on her face.

"Is my father here? He isn't upstairs. I've searched everywhere for him."

That triggered Kaia's own worries. Had something happened to the inspector? The possibility that he might be hurt somewhere there made fear flow through her.

"We need to find him," Kaia said. "He might be hurt somewhere. He might be…"

She didn't want to say the word "dead" because even speaking that fear aloud might make it real.

"If he's not in the house, maybe he was following the killer?" Em guessed. "But without calling for us?"

Kaia hoped that was what it was, because the alternative was that the shadow had taken him out of there, either to kill him or to hold him captive. No, Kaia had to hope that he had simply gone out after the killer.

Even that was a worrying thought, though, because why wasn't the inspector back? Why hadn't he tried to wake them all to help him? He had to know by now that Kaia or Em represented his best chance of help against one of the shadows.

Had he run after the killer only for them to turn on him and hurt him? Had he run out into the city and gotten lost? In a city with so many shadows around, even that was not a comforting thought. Yes, the inspector could fight, and probably had his pistol with him, but against the shadows, would either of those things truly be enough?

"We need to get out there and find him," Kaia said.

Her aunt nodded. "I agree. I'm very worried that something may happen to Sebastian if we do not manage to locate him soon."

Kaia needed no further encouragement. She ran for the front door to the safehouse, and then out into the city, determined to find the inspector if he was there to be found.

CHAPTER TEN

Em went with the others out into the street, trying to catch any glimpse of the inspector. She scanned the street around her in case he had come out only to be attacked, and also to make sure that she and the others weren't about to be ambushed. While her aunt might have assumed that she was the one in charge because of her experience fighting against the shadows, Em knew that it was she herself and Kaia who could provide the best warning that they were coming, along with possessing the best natural weapons with which to fight them.

They had to find the inspector, and they had to do it quickly, before anything could happen to him. He wasn't quite the father figure to her that he was to Kaia, because Em *had* an adoptive father in the form of the British ambassador to France, but he had still done a lot to protect and help her. The thought that something might have happened to him worried her a lot.

She and the others checked the length of the street carefully for any sign of the inspector, then circled around, checking the nearest side streets. Around them, Athens was just waking up, with people leaving their homes to go to whatever work they had in the city, all dressed in a very different fashion from London or Paris. Here, the heat meant much lighter clothing, rather than stuffy suits or heavy layers of dresses. Em suspected that might make the inspector a little easier to pick out if they spotted him, because it was unlikely that he would take off the long frock coat he usually wore for anything.

He would be distinctive enough in any case, with his height and his military bearing. Even at a distance, Em was confident that she would be able to pick him out from a crowd. Assuming that he was able to walk among the crowd, and not slumped in some back street, bleeding from a wound inflicted by one of the shadow possessed.

Em knew that was why they were checking the side streets one by one, moving up and down them carefully, scouring each doorway they came to as if they might find the inspector slumped down in it. Yet it seemed so slow that it was impossible not to think that they were wasting time. Every street they looked down without success was another minute or two in which the inspector might be bleeding to death somewhere.

We could try our powers, Em sent to Kaia. *Maybe we will be able to find him the way we did with the shadowseer.*

He's not *a shadowseer, though,* Kaia replied. *Or a shadow. We won't be able to see him.*

We have to at least try. Em held out her hand pointedly to her sister. They had to attempt everything, even if it only had the smallest chance of succeeding.

After a moment or two, Kaia relented, putting her hand in Em's, the relic between them in an attempt to boost their powers the way it had before. Em still felt a little resentful toward Aunt Keris that she hadn't thought it was safe to leave the orb in Em's care, but at least when Kaia had it, it meant that the two of them could use it.

Their powers flared up, and now that Em had been to Venice, now that she had felt the extent of her powers when alone, she felt the unequal nature of those powers. She and Kaia were twins, identical in almost every respect except this one. When it came to their powers, Em was by far the weaker of the two. If the average shadowseer had a puddle of power on which to draw, Em's power was a lake, but Kaia… Kaia was like a deep, unfathomable sea.

Combined, those powers burst out, letting them see over the city as they had before. Em loved this facet of their powers, although it lacked the sheer ferocious energy with which Kaia could send people flying or destroy shadows utterly. There was something special about getting to see more than anyone else could, and about learning everything there was to know about a person or place.

Em could see the city, see the presence of shadows gathered around the Acropolis, more than she wanted to think about. She could see others, dotted around the city.

Crucially, though, she thought that she could see one moving away from the safehouse at speed.

There, Em sent to Kaia.

That's a shadow, not the inspector.

And why is the inspector likely to have left? Em insisted.

Because he's chasing after the killer, Kaia replied, finally getting it.

Em pulled back, feeling herself come back into herself. Around her, she could see the others still searching.

"This way," she said. "The shadow is going this way!"

She led the way through the streets, just assuming that the others would follow. It never occurred to Em that they wouldn't. Sometimes, the most important thing was simply to act, not to wait. So she plunged through the streets of Athens, trying to follow after the shadow in the hope that the inspector was chasing the shadow too and that this would get them to him.

At the very least, if they caught up to the shadow, they could force it to tell them what it had done with the inspector. Em glanced around and saw the others hurrying in her wake as Em wove her way through the crowds on the streets, trying to get closer to where she and Kaia had seen the shadow.

The only problem now was that the image was fading.

"We need to find it again," Em said, holding out her hand to Kaia.

Kaia took her hand again, but their power didn't rise this time, as if it were reluctant to be called again so soon. Em had definitely found that in the past, with their power being a fickle thing that would only come when they absolutely needed it, and that would fail if overused. Yet now, they needed it more than ever, and Em could feel the reserves of it. It was frustrating, but not as frustrating as the fact that they hadn't found the inspector yet.

"Which way?" Olivia asked, obviously assuming that the two of them had seen the correct way to go again.

Kaia shook her head. "We didn't see anything. This way of using our power is trickier than just blasting away shadows."

Em wondered if her sister had ever thought at the start of all this that she would come to accept what she could do so fully.

"We'll have to go back to searching," Aunt Keris said. "Stick together."

"We'll cover more ground if we split up," Em pointed out. She gestured to the streets around them. They were standing on a major thoroughfare, with a main trunk continuing straight, and branches off to both their left and right. "There are only three ways they could have gone, so if we split up, we can cover all three."

"And leave ourselves vulnerable if the shadows attack us," Aunt Keris replied.

"We have the skills to protect ourselves," Em insisted. "Kaia and I can both cast out a shadow. I could go right with Casper, Olivia and Kaia could go left together, and you could search straight on."

Before Venice, Em would have insisted on teaming up with her sister, but she and the young shadowseer had worked well together there, and… well, it would be good to snatch even the briefest chance to spend time with him. She still had memories of having to dance close to him, hidden by a mask to avoid being caught by shadows back in Venice.

"No," Aunt Keris said. "Absolutely not. The danger is too great."

Em wondered if she meant the danger of the shadows or the kind of "dangers" her chaperones back in school warned about that made it impossible to be alone with a boy. Either way, Em wasn't about to accept it. She and Casper made a good team, and they *would* cover more ground if they split up.

"You don't just get to forbid it," Em said. "You're not in charge here, and we risk missing the inspector if we don't split up."

"I am both your aunt and the head of a whole chapter of shadowseers," Aunt Keris snapped. "And I don't have time for your rebellious streak right now, Emmeline. Not when Sebastian might be in danger. I need you to do as I say."

Em wasn't about to simply go along with that. Not from her. Not now.

"I might trust your authority more if you hadn't brought us here to sacrifice our lives in this ritual of yours," Em shot back.

"How many times? I have no intention of you performing the ritual. We can shut down the portal without it!"

Em was about to retort that her aunt didn't know that for sure; that, frankly, she didn't know as much about powers and portals as either Em or Kaia. That Em was sick of someone they'd only met a few weeks ago acting as if she'd been there for their entire lives, rather than hanging back, letting them believe that they had no one.

Even as she wound up to say it, Em knew that it would be the kind of thing that couldn't be unsaid, the kind of thing that would create a small fissure between the two of them that could never truly be closed.

Olivia must have sensed that things were getting out of hand, because she stepped between them.

"No one wants my father back more than I do," she said. "But arguing isn't going to get him back. And I don't think he would want us to split up. He wouldn't want you risking your safety for his, Em. We will find him, but we will do it together."

Em was still frustrated. Couldn't Olivia see that doing it that way would be too slow? That it risked losing the inspector completely?

"Olivia..." Em began, and then paused as she saw someone in the crowd.

It was a young woman, probably no older than Olivia, maybe as young as her and Kaia. She was dark haired and very pretty, with wide eyes and high cheekbones. She was wearing a light, flowing dress and sandals that seemed almost deliberately old-fashioned.

Two things caught Em's eye when it came to the girl. One was the way she wandered around aimlessly, looking confused, staring from one side of the street to another as if she weren't quite sure what was happening.

The other was the fact that her arms were covered in blood. The combination seemed clear: this was the vessel the shadow had been using when it killed Nasos.

"There's a girl," Em said. The others obviously hadn't spotted her. "Look."

Em pointed, and too late, she realized that pointing was exactly the wrong thing to do in that situation. The girl was looking their way, which meant that she saw a whole group of strangers armed with an odd assortment of weapons turn their attention her way.

Almost the moment Em pointed, the girl turned to run, setting off through the crowd as fast as her legs would carry her.

Em knew that the girl represented their best chance of finding the inspector, and that they couldn't afford to let her get away. Without waiting to see what the others would do, she set off in pursuit.

CHAPTER ELEVEN

Kaia saw the girl as Em pointed, saw the blood on her hands, and understood what it had to mean: that this was the person who had killed Nasos.

When the girl turned to run, Kaia wasn't entirely surprised. She *definitely* wasn't surprised when Em set off in pursuit without hesitating, sprinting after her. Kaia knew that she couldn't leave her sister to face the potential danger alone, so she ran after Em with the others following. She just hoped that Em wasn't going to jump off a roof this time.

They weren't chasing over the roofs of houses, though, but through the crowds on the streets of Athens. That meant that there was no chance of falling to their deaths this time, but there *were* people in the way, shouting as Kaia ran past, getting in the way without meaning to and slowing her down.

The girl running away had an advantage in the crowd, because she could run through the gaps between people, shove them out of the way, and by the time they started to react, she was already moving on. That left Em and Kaia trying to dodge around increasingly annoyed pedestrians, weaving between them, dodging past horses and carts, trying not to let the chaos slow them down.

Kaia glanced back and saw Aunt Keris having to shove her way through the crowd with Casper and Olivia. Because she and Em were smaller and slighter, though, Kaia could dodge through the gaps between people, bouncing off them rather than trying to push them aside, just making sure that she kept moving.

The hardest part was keeping her eyes fixed on the fleeing girl, because she moved almost randomly through the busy streets, pinballing from person to person, hard to keep track of. She was short and slender enough that she disappeared easily behind people, while Kaia's own lack of height meant that she couldn't see over the heads of the crowd to track her.

Still, Kaia did her best to keep up with both the fleeing girl and with Em, following as they darted down a side street, seeing the girl tip over a rain barrel into their path. Kaia hurdled over it, determined to keep going.

She had to throw herself back then as a horse and cart pulled out of a courtyard in her path, the cart piled high with bottles of some unknown liquid.

"Hey!" the driver bellowed at her in Greek. "Keep out of the way if you don't want to get run over!"

Kaia didn't slow down, though. Instead, she clambered up onto the cart and then leapt down the far side, continuing to follow the young woman they were chasing.

"Thief!" Em shouted out, ahead of Kaia. "Thief!"

It was a clever move. People who wouldn't have interfered before now started to step into the young woman's path, blocking her way. If Em had shouted out that she was a murderer, they might have stepped back out of fear, but for a thief, they were prepared to try to intervene.

For the briefest moment, Kaia found her memories flashing back to the brush with the law that had first brought her to Inspector Pinsley's attention. She'd been accused of theft when she hadn't done it, and the fear that came with that had been almost overwhelming. Kaia wasn't sure how she felt then about her sister using that kind of tactic now.

At the same time, though, this girl had probably just killed someone. Calling her a thief didn't sound so bad in comparison to that.

None of the people in the girl's path managed to grab her, though, only funnel her down more and more side streets. Kaia had to keep looking back, hoping that her aunt, Olivia, and Casper could still at least see her. They were further back in the crowd, still having to push through. She held up a hand to wave to them, pointing to the next street, hoping that they would see which way Kaia was going. She didn't want them to become lost, not when there was still a chance that this was all leading them into an ambush.

In spite of that worry, Kaia kept running. Maybe because of it, because she knew that Em wasn't about to slow down and she didn't want her sister running into danger without her.

Finally, the three of them turned into a small alley that turned out to be a dead end. A wall sat across it, easily ten feet high. The young woman ran down to the end of it, pressing at the bricks of that wall as if she might somehow find a way through them. Then she whirled at bay, pulling out a knife that must have been the one she used to kill Nasos.

"Stay back," she said in Greek. "I see you, monsters. I know you're here to kill me. I see everything."

Em looked as though she was ready for a fight, but Kaia put a hand on her shoulder. Kaia couldn't feel the presence of any shadows in this girl. If they'd had control of her before, they didn't have it now.

"We're not here to hurt you," Kaia said.

"The gods whisper to me, you know," the girl said. "They've done it since I was a child. I've always been able to hear them: Artemis, Demeter... all of them."

Kaia saw Em look over to her with a frown.

This girl is obviously mad.

It may be a side effect of having had the shadows inside her, Kaia pointed out.

We've met people who were taken by them, Em replied. *And* they *didn't start talking about hearing Ancient Greek gods.*

"You look like you're talking to each other," the young woman said. "But I can't hear the words. Then other times, I hear words, even though people don't say them. I see the meanings in the clouds and the flight of birds."

"What's your name?" Kaia asked. She did her best to ignore the knife still held tightly in the girl's hand, and the blood on her forearms that must have come from Nasos.

"Names? Yes, things have names. If you understand their names, you understand them. The god who came to stay in me wouldn't give me its name. Only now, I think it might have been a demon or a fury, because of what it made me do."

She was aware of the shadow that had been inside her, then.

"What did it make you do?" Em asked her, presumably looking for some kind of confession.

"It made me sit on a fountain and..." The girl shook her head though, looking pained. "No, no, I can't, I mustn't. It wasn't real. It can't be real. It's all just a dream."

There had been a fountain in the square where the shadowseers were killed. Had this been the one at the heart of that, the one who had lured the shadowseers in to their deaths? Nasos had said that he'd been able to feel the shadow possessing the young woman from streets away, such was its power.

That shadow was obviously gone now, though.

"What's your name?" Kaia tried again. "I'm Kaia, and this is my sister, Em."

"Cassiopeia," the girl said, and then looked slightly confused, as if having to check if that was right. "Yes. Cassiopeia."

"Will you put the knife down, please, Cassiopeia?" Kaia asked.

"Are you going to kill me?" she asked. She sounded suddenly very scared, and also as if she couldn't imagine them behaving any other way. "I saw you all, and I killed... I killed your friend."

"That wasn't you, though," Em said. "That was the shadow."

My guess is that her madness made it impossible for her to keep the shadow out, Kaia sent. *I saw it in Bedlam.*

"The shadow," Cassiopeia said. "Yes, that's a good name for it. All big and dark and following me everywhere. But then I was the shadow, and it was the person. It was like I could only watch. It took over my whole life. It said I'd never had any fun, and it made me do... everything."

She put the knife down, almost as if she were scared it might break if she dropped it. Kaia saw Em dart forward to pick it up, but Kaia went to Cassiopeia, putting an arm around her shoulders.

That was when Aunt Keris, Olivia, and Casper finally caught up, all of them looking as though they expected to find Em, Kaia, and Cassiopeia caught up in a bloody battle. They all had the weapons they had taken from the shadowseers' safehouse, and at the sight of them, Kaia felt Cassiopeia pull back.

"No, you tricked me. They're here to kill me!"

"No, they aren't," Kaia assured her. She looked over to her aunt and the others. "Put your weapons away, all of you. Cassiopeia isn't a threat."

"Is she the one who killed Nasos?" Aunt Keris asked.

"While there was a shadow in her," Kaia insisted. "*Look* at her, Aunt Keris. She's scared and she's confused."

"She thinks she talks to Ancient Greek gods," Em said, bluntly.

Kaia saw the moment when her aunt relented slightly, obviously seeing, as Kaia could see, that Cassiopeia was another victim of the shadows, not some terrifying, evil figure.

"But does she know where my father is?" Olivia asked. That reminded Kaia of the purpose of all of this. They might have found Nasos's killer, technically, but they hadn't been looking for her; they'd been trying to find the inspector.

"Do you?" Kaia asked. "Do you know where he is?"

"The man? The man who was in the place you were?" Cassiopeia said.

"Yes," Kaia replied. "What happened to him, Cassiopeia? Did he chase you?"

"Did you hurt him?" Aunt Keris asked.

Cassiopeia started shaking her head sharply. "No, no. No, no, no. No, I didn't. I didn't."

"Did the shadow inside you?" Em asked.

It was an important question. Cassiopeia might think that she hadn't done anything, might say that she hadn't, because she didn't see it as her when the shadow had been in control.

"No," Cassiopeia said. "No, it didn't use me to hurt him. I don't know what happened. We went out of there, and... I don't know, I don't remember."

"Don't remember, or won't say?" Aunt Keris demanded.

Kaia gave her aunt a pointed look. "Being harsh with her won't help."

Her aunt nodded. "You're right, of course. The question, though, is what we do next."

"Do we keep searching?" Casper asked.

Aunt Keris had a pained expression on her face as she shook her head. "I don't think we're getting anywhere by looking blindly. It seems clear that Sebastian is nowhere near the safehouse. We need to work out what happened to him, but we can't do that here."

"You're giving up?" Olivia asked. Kaia could hear the concern for her father.

"We're not giving up," Aunt Keris assured her. "But we need to think of a way of finding the inspector that might actually work. We need to think, and the best place to do that is back at the safehouse."

"And what do we do with her?" Em asked, nodding toward Cassiopeia.

That was an important question. Kaia had seen how confused Cassiopeia was, and how distressed she was by the things that had happened. It seemed cruel to just leave her there, covered in blood, especially when the shadows had already targeted her once.

"We bring her with us," Aunt Keris said. "We will be able to help her better than anyone else, and my hope is that she may be able to help us find out more, even if she doesn't think she knows anything now."

CHAPTER TWELVE

They returned to the safehouse, and Kaia's heart was in her mouth as she realized that Nasos's body was still there in the dining room. They'd run out looking for answers, trying to find the inspector, and they hadn't had enough time to even consider what to do about Nasos.

It seemed that Aunt Keris *had* thought about it, though.

"Casper, can you take care of the body?" she said.

"You're just going to… what? Bury him?" Em asked, sounding slightly shocked.

"We cannot bring the police into shadowseer affairs," Aunt Keris said. "It would place them and us in danger. We can only continue the fight against the shadows when we are not dragged out into the open."

Even so, it made Kaia feel a little uncomfortable.

"Then there is the question of the girl," Aunt Keris said, nodding to Cassiopeia. "If the police become involved, how long do you think it will be before they decide that she is guilty?"

"But it wasn't me!" Cassiopeia insisted. "It was the thing, the demon, the shadow!"

"We know that," Olivia said, in a calming tone, holding up a hand to forestall her objections. "But if the police get involved, then they won't believe that."

"They would assume that the girl killed her in a fit of madness," Aunt Keris said. "At best, she would be locked away in whatever institutions they have here. At worst, she might find herself executed for the crime."

Kaia knew that it was far too possible. She had seen in London how swift and brutal the legal system could be. The police here in Athens certainly wouldn't understand the idea that a shadow had possessed Cassiopeia and forced her to act as she did.

"All right," Em said, also conceding the point. "I don't like it, but all right."

"I'll take care of things," Casper said, moving off into the dining room.

Meanwhile, Aunt Keris led the rest of them through into a white-walled drawing room lined with the same pictures as the rest of the house, seeming to mingle Greek myths with the actions of the shadowseers, hinting at a long history for their kind. Kaia could see a picture that appeared to show a pair of twins, striding out together among a set of ruins, light flaring from them as darkness surrounded them.

Aunt Keris took a seat in a large, broad armchair. Em and Kaia settled on a couch with Cassiopeia between them. The girl seemed to be at least vaguely comfortable there, although her eyes still darted around warily.

Olivia briefly went into the small kitchen of the safehouse, coming out with food, water, and a couple of cloths. Kaia wasn't hungry. She wanted to find a way to locate the inspector.

"Could you try your powers again?" Olivia asked her and Em.

"I don't think it will do much good," Kaia said. "We can see where the shadows are in the city, and shadowseers, but the inspector isn't either of those. We just can't see him."

They needed another way of finding him.

"Cassiopeia," Aunt Keris said. "I think that we need to ask you some questions."

"I don't know where the tall man went," Cassiopeia said. "I didn't see. I know he talked to us, but I wasn't allowed to hear it. One moment, it was like I was locked in a room having to watch the world through a window, the next, I was out there in the street, and the thing in me was gone. The gods won't even tell me why. They just whisper and murmur and it's…"

Kaia saw her start to cry, and put a hand on her arm. She remembered the blood there too late, and then realized what the water and cloths were for that Olivia had brought out. Gently, Kaia did her best to wash some of the blood from the girl's arm.

"Can you tell us anything else?" Kaia asked. "I know you don't know anything about the inspector, but maybe something about the way the shadows are doing what they're doing?"

It wasn't just that there was still the huge threat of the portal hanging over this, and that it was due to be the full moon tonight. It was also that a part of Kaia still wanted to believe that the inspector was missing because he had learned something so vital that it couldn't wait for him to investigate it. That he had gone after Cassiopeia, spoken to her, and simply had to act. She'd even said that they'd spoken, so it was possible, wasn't it?

She understood the other possibilities, though. He might have been possessed by a shadow. That seemed unlikely, though, when he had resisted them before. He didn't have the kinds of weaknesses that

63

normally let them in; he was too strong for that. He might still have been kidnapped by some other shadow possessed. Maybe the shadow had used Cassiopeia to lure him into a trap?

"I don't know," Cassiopeia said. "I don't... there was something. A place. A house. I'd never had a house before. And suddenly I had a house. I had money. Or it did. That was where..." Her tears only intensified.

"What happened there?" Aunt Keris asked, but Cassiopeia shook her head.

Kaia decided to try a different approach.

"Do you remember where the house is?" she asked.

Cassiopeia nodded, but then looked at her with something like panic. "Don't make me go back there. Please don't make me go back there."

"You don't have to go back anywhere," Aunt Keris said. "You can stay here. You'll be safe here. But we do need you to tell us where that house is. Whatever's going on there, it seems like our best chance of finding the inspector."

*

The house was grander than Kaia had expected it would be, a large house in what appeared to be one of Athens's wealthier districts. Its white-painted walls rose three stories high, while a gate at the side suggested access to gardens.

They went through that, with Kaia and the others following her aunt. Casper had stayed behind to guard the safehouse and Cassiopeia, since it probably wasn't safe to leave her there alone when she had no defenses to keep out the shadows.

The space beyond the gate was a broad paved plaza, with plants set in large stone pots and statues standing in between them. The whole place seemed wealthy in a way completely at odds with the strange mad girl they'd found down in the city.

Was the inspector here? Had he come here to search? Kaia could only hope so as the four of them made their way to a side door and Aunt Keris bent to pick the lock. The lock gave way quickly, the door swinging open to let them inside.

The interior of the house was a place of opulent wealth, with a huge central room on the ground floor, marble columns supporting the ceiling, and broad couches scattered there, either for sitting on or sleeping on, Kaia wasn't sure which.

In between them lay discarded bottles and bowls, pipes and packets that suggested that the shadow had been determined to try every possible human pleasure while it had a physical body. Kaia thought that she could see bloodstains in one corner, and there were definitely beautiful clothes scattered across the floor, as if they'd simply been tried and abandoned.

"What is all this?" Em said.

Olivia answered. "Excess. Pure excess. Someone trying everything they could, knowing that they could always abandon Cassiopeia's body afterwards."

No wonder the young woman hadn't wanted to come back here.

"We need to search the house," Aunt Keris said. "We need to find any sign that Sebastian has been here, and where he might have gone next. Split up and call if you see *anything* unusual."

They spread out around the ground floor, but Kaia had the feeling that anything truly important wasn't going to be there, so close to where people came into the house, and where the shadow had obviously dedicated itself to trying out all the possibilities of the flesh.

She headed for a broad staircase instead. How had the shadow gotten this place? Had it simply taken it, the way it took bodies, or had it used other shadows to force people to give up their money? It seemed impossible to work out for sure, and for the moment at least, Kaia's focus was on trying to find anything that might tell her where the inspector was.

She headed upstairs, and now there were rooms branching off. The first one Kaia tried was a bedroom, at least as large as the entire rectory Kaia had lived in back in London. That, strangely, had artists' easels set up across most of it, with strange, weird paintings, half of them in shades of black and gray, as if the shadow were trying to find a way to paint its world.

The next door was worse. That room was largely empty, except for a chair set at its heart, bolted to the floor. Ropes hung loose from its arms, and a table at the side held the kind of tools that Kaia might have associated with a carpenter or a blacksmith, only most of them had blood on them.

She backed out of that room in a hurry.

Should she call her aunt? Was *that* enough to bring her and the others running? A truly awful thought came to Kaia: what if that was the inspector's blood? No, she told herself, it couldn't be. There had been no time in which to do all of this to him. That gave Kaia a brief sense of relief, but her worry returned with the thought that she still didn't know what had happened to the inspector. He could be in at least this much danger somewhere else.

That made Kaia press on into the third room there. There were more easels set up there, but *these* didn't hold the shadow's attempts at artwork. Instead, they held chalk boards, each of them covered in…

Well, Kaia wasn't entirely sure *what* they were. Some of it looked like math, but it was far more advanced than anything they'd bothered to teach her back in the orphanage. Kaia suspected that it was far more advanced than anything taught in any school in England, probably in any of its universities. Some of the symbols seemed to be more like runes, or even some kind of abstract art. Kaia thought she recognized some of them. She'd seen them before on the portals she'd come across in Paris and Rome.

There were drawings there too, what looked like a plan of a network of runes around a portal. This wasn't leading them to the inspector, but she was pretty sure it was something her aunt would want to see.

"Aunt Keris! Up here!" Kaia called out.

It was only a matter of seconds before her aunt and the others came running in. Kaia saw her aunt looking around the room as if she expected to find the inspector there, hurt or dead. Her worried expression didn't improve as she took in the contents of the room.

"This looks like preparations for whatever ritual they're going to do to open the portal," she said. Kaia saw her touch some of the symbols. "These are shadowseer marks. They're trying to work out how to adapt the ritual site. And judging by these plans, they have a good idea of how to do it."

Kaia saw her aunt grow pale.

"What is it?" she asked.

"I believe I can understand what they're trying to do," Aunt Keris said. "They aren't just trying to open a portal. They have proven that they can do that anywhere."

"Then what?" Em asked.

"The ritual is designed to weaken and destroy the shadows. It appears that they are trying to subvert it, *invert* it," Aunt Keris said. "They are trying to use the power of the ritual site to make shadows stronger as they come through the portal."

"How *much* stronger?" Olivia asked with a shudder.

"Potentially… potentially they might be strong enough to take people over without them having some kind of weakness to exploit," Aunt Keris said.

That thought filled Kaia with horror. Suddenly, this wasn't just another portal. This was an invasion, a colonization. It was… it was the end of humanity as they knew it.

Chapter 13

Mr. Illingworth stepped off the boat, looking around at Athens, less than impressed. Books had it that this was the cradle of civilization, a place of beauty and wonder, philosophy and history.

Mostly, to Mr. Illingworth, it looked small. Certainly compared to the scale and modernity of London, or Rome, it seemed like a backwater. Certainly, there were still enough complexities here that Illingworth would be able to get more notes for his ledger while he was here, but compared to anywhere else…

No, he really couldn't see why a mind like Pinsley's would have brought him to a place like this. Paris, yes, that had made sense. From what Illingworth understood, his daughter had been there, and in any case the political situation was delicate. Munich… it wasn't the political hotbed that Prussia was, but from what Illingworth understood there had at least been significant figures there. That endeavor had resulted in the death of a prince, no less. As for Rome, was there anywhere *more* relevant at the moment, with the attempts to unite Italy going on around it?

Illingworth had followed Pinsley's efforts in *those* places with a certain amount of fascination, even respect. He'd quickly established that the detective was a man like him, able to see the patterns running beneath things, and had assumed that he was making calculated interventions designed to affect the wider picture in ways that would ultimately be beneficial to him. Or perhaps to some notion of what was right, given that the detective seemed annoyingly encumbered by a conscience.

Yet Illingworth couldn't understand what he might be trying to achieve *here*. This was the kind of place a young man might head to on the grand tour, or an antiquarian might travel seeking objects to bring back to London to impress. It did not fit with what Illingworth had seen of the rest of Pinsley's travels.

Still, he would work it out.

"I have made arrangements for my stay," Illingworth said to a porter in perfect Greek, handing over the larger of his two bags of luggage. The smaller hold-all he kept on his shoulder. He held out a few drachma coins for the man. "See that this is taken to this address."

"Of course, sir," the man said. "Perhaps I should take your umbrella? There is no rain forecast."

"It will stay with me." Illingworth tapped the sharp end on the ground and let his tone go cold. "If anything is missing from my bag, I will hold you personally responsible."

He could see the fear in the man's eyes. Most people were easy to frighten. And while he had the man frightened, it seemed like a very good moment to start asking questions.

"I am looking for some… friends of mine in the city," he said, as if he had friends rather than carefully calculated acquaintances. "They would have arrived on a boat yesterday. A small group, led by a tall man with a lean face and mutton chop whiskers."

The porter cocked his head to one side. "There was someone like that. What's it worth to you?"

Illingworth calculated quickly. He suspected that if he gave over more money, the man would only give him part of the story, and would probably have a few of his friends try to rob Illingworth later. Not that it would be a real threat to him, but it might slow his investigation down. No, it was better to deal with all of this now.

So he took the point of his umbrella and set it against the man's foot, pressing down just enough to push through the leather of his boot. The porter seemed so surprised that he actually dropped Illingworth's bag, but that was all right. Illingworth had anticipated it, and had his own hand waiting to catch it.

"I think the question you have to ask yourself," he said, "is what is the continued ability to walk worth to *you*?"

"There were six of them," the porter said hurriedly. "I thought they were a family, maybe. A man and a woman in their forties. An older girl, two girls of maybe seventeen, must have been twins, and a boy, although maybe he was a family friend or something."

"Where did they *go*?" Illingworth asked him.

"They… they were asking questions about some fountain here in the city," the porter said. "Psyche and Eros. That's all I know, I swear."

A part of Illingworth wanted to stab his umbrella through the man's foot anyway, just to make a point, but he suspected that would cause more problems than it solved. He didn't want what passed for the authorities in Athens hunting for him and getting in the way of his investigation.

"There," he said instead. "That wasn't so difficult."

He walked away. He could have asked for directions to the fountain, but Illingworth wasn't sure that he would have trusted anything the porter told him right then. Instead, he walked, carrying his bag and doing his best to ignore the heat, until he found a small café, run by a woman in her fifties with a rotund figure, dark hair, and quite piercing blue eyes. She looked at Illingworth with the kind of interest he generally didn't trust, knowing that all such entanglements usually led to pain. That was a lesson his quarry should have learned too, given his wife's death at the hands of a madman.

"I'm new in the city," Illingworth said, as he took possession of a cup of strong Greek coffee and a slice of orange cake. "I like to know about the cities I visit, and I guess that you must hear *all* the gossip."

"Well, people do like to talk," the café owner said, with a smile that suggested that she was happy to show off to Illingworth. "Although things are strange in Athens at the moment."

"Strange? In what way?" If necessary, of course, he would use threats to get the information he required, but it was easier for now to play the part of the intrigued traveler, trying to learn more about a new city.

"There have been a lot of people behaving strangely, doing things they wouldn't normally do. There have been people wandering around in the dark, and screams in the night. Something is happening, but no one is quite sure what."

Hmm, maybe there was a reason for the inspector to be there after all.

"Can you give me directions to a plaza with a fountain that has a statue of Psyche and Eros at its center?" Illingworth said. "I am meant to meet some friends there now that I'm in the city, but I have realized that I don't know the way."

"Of course," the café owner said. She came to the front of the café, pointing. "You go up that way, turn left when you reach the taverna with the blue door. You can't miss it. But I hope you'll stay for some more coffee before you—"

Illingworth was already striding away without a word. The key was to catch his quarry, not to try to make friends in Athens. He made his way quickly up the street, determined to find the place the inspector had been looking for.

If it came to it, Illingworth would comb the city for him block by block. He would pay informants and listen to every possible rumor in the hope of finding Pinsley. The problem with that, though, was that it would be slow. It would take time that Illingworth might not have, when it seemed that his quarry never stayed in a city, or even a country, for more than a few days at a time.

No, it was better to follow the more direct route to his target. The inspector was looking into something, and so Illingworth would follow that trail until it led to him.

He headed for the taverna, and his sharp eyes took in the damage to one of its shutters. Had there been a particularly out of control bar fight, or had something else happened there? The inspector and his young companion seemed to have a knack for attracting danger. Maybe they had been involved.

If Illingworth got nowhere in the square, he would ask there about them.

For now, though, the square seemed to be the best place to look. Illingworth found it easily enough, thanks to the directions he'd been given, taking in its enclosed sides, and the statue atop the fountain at its heart. Briefly, his memory supplied him with the details of the myth, of the human woman Psyche who angered the gods with her beauty and who was meant to be pricked by Eros's arrows to make her fall in love with an ugly, monstrous man, but with whom Eros fell in love instead. Illingworth had crammed knowledge of such things into his head the way he'd acquired other potentially useful knowledge. There was always a subset of Harrow and Eton educated men in the British establishment who valued such affectations of intelligence ahead of its reality. Discuss Descartes or the cricket with them down at their club and they would forgive almost anything.

From the statue, Illingworth's eyes moved to the rest of the small square. There were a few people here now, but it seemed a quiet sort of place, and there was no sign of the missing inspector.

There *were* signs that indicated a violent struggle, though. Illingworth walked the confines of the square, taking in the bloodstains and the bullet holes, the cracks and the scuff marks. Eleven people had come to this place and converged on the fountain, then died, taken by surprise by unknown foes. A twelfth, judging by the traces, had managed to escape.

Was the whole affair something that Pinsley had been involved in? Had he been one of the people to die? Had he *watched* them die? Perhaps he had been the one they had been surrounding?

No, Illingworth chastised himself. Of course he hadn't. Anyone, or at least anyone with Illingworth's skills, could see that the bloodstains were a good two days old, when it seemed unlikely that Pinsley would have gotten to Athens before yesterday. In any case, Illingworth simply didn't believe that the inspector was the kind of man who would cold-bloodedly lure people to their deaths.

It was yet another difference between them.

If Pinsley wasn't behind this, though, that left a more interesting possibility: that he was seeking to *investigate* what had happened here. That meant that trying to follow that investigation should eventually lead to the inspector. It was simply a matter of making the appropriate deductions.

Illingworth went around the square again, wanting to be sure that he got all the information that was there for him to find. He checked every corner carefully. He was still checking when he saw a small group of people come into the square.

The first thing to catch his attention was the fact that they were speaking English.

"I don't get what we're doing here, Kaia," one of them said.

The second thing was that name, because it was unusual enough that it seemed unlikely that Illingworth would run into someone with it simply by accident.

"We're retracing the inspector's steps, Em."

It was them, the people who had traveled here with the inspector. Or at least, four of the five: one woman in her forties, a younger woman of perhaps nineteen, and two young ladies who appeared identical to one another. One of them was Kaia, the girl who Hutton claimed had dragged Pinsley away to France, while the other could only be the twin sister his operatives in Rome had mentioned.

Yet there seemed to be no sign of Pinsley with them. That was disappointing, and made the possibility of direct action less helpful. Illingworth briefly considered the idea of perhaps taking them as hostages, knowing that the inspector would almost certainly give himself up for them, but he decided to reserve that as a plan B.

It was easier to watch and wait. If Illingworth was careful, then he would be able to follow them all the way back to the inspector. Once they led him there, then it would be a simple matter to capture Pinsley for a return to London. And if the others tried to interfere... well, Illingworth had no compunction whatsoever about killing them.

CHAPTER THIRTEEN

Kaia led the way back toward the square with the fountain in it, determined to start finding answers that might lead them to the inspector. With the shadows due to open their portal in the city tonight, they only had a matter of hours in which to find him.

"Why are we going back this way?" Em asked as Kaia kept walking.

"I'm inclined to ask that as well, Kaia," Aunt Keris said. "I am willing to go along with it in the absence of better ideas to find Sebastian, but there seems to be little purpose to revisiting a space where we have already been."

Kaia did her best to explain as she walked.

"I'm just thinking about what the inspector would do. Whenever we haven't known what to do in the past, he's wanted to go back to the start of things and look over all the evidence again. Well, that fountain is the start of things here."

"It's reasonable," Olivia said. "And there's also the chance that my father will do the same thing."

"If he's trying to follow leads on the case," Aunt Keris pointed out.

"He might be," Kaia said. "He's tried to cut me out of cases in the past, to try to keep me safe."

She saw her aunt frown. "Do you think that's what he's doing now, Kaia?"

Kaia had to shake her head. The inspector had tried to protect her less as he'd started to realize how skilled and powerful she was, how much she could actually help. Especially after the attempt of the bounty hunters to capture him in Rome, Kaia couldn't imagine the inspector trying to keep her and the others out of this. Not when he knew that they might be able to help.

"No," she had to admit. "Not unless he found something that he thought only one person could investigate. Not unless there was something so urgent that he felt as though he *had* to go after it."

He must have gone out chasing after Cassiopeia, but she'd told them that he'd found her. The only reason he might have kept going was if he'd thought of something else, if something she'd said had sparked some hint of inspiration.

Whatever the reason, the inspector wasn't there, and all Kaia could think of was to search the square again. There were a few people in there today, some making their way to work, some hanging around to talk, a few looking at the fountain admiringly.

Kaia tried to look for the blood traces that the inspector had worked from, finding a couple of them, not that they told her anything.

"I think you need the inspector's powers of deduction for all of this to mean anything," Em said.

That was the hard part of all of this. Kaia had talents that let her fight against the shadows, and she'd managed to deal with some very dangerous situations, but that wasn't the same thing as being able to work out the finest details of a situation just from a glance.

"I'm not sure that there's anything new that we can learn here," Aunt Keris said. "We should return to the safehouse and try to proceed from there. Maybe if we ask about the inspector around the city, we'll be able to find some hint of where he is."

"It sounds like a long shot," Olivia said.

"It will take time," Aunt Keris agreed, "but it still gives us the best chance we have right now of finding him."

Kaia had to agree, and as her aunt started to lead the way back out of the small plaza, she followed, hoping that the four of them would be able to find something that might point them in the direction the inspector had gone.

They set off back down the streets of the city, moving against the general flow of the crowd. Kaia looked around as she walked, trying to find any sign that the inspector might have come that way again, any sign that he might have been trying to find new evidence in the case.

She saw something else, instead, something odd.

There's a man walking behind us, she sent to Em, wanting to be sure that it was real before she said anything to her aunt.

There are a lot of men in the street, Em said. *Most of them are just walking to work, or to a store, or something.*

But this *one isn't walking the same way the others are,* Kaia insisted. The man she could see seemed to be picking his way through the crowd behind them, keeping a careful distance behind them, but keeping his eyes on them. He didn't look like the others there either. He was dressed in a light-colored linen suit, wearing a broad-brimmed hat, and walking while leaning on a wooden-handled umbrella.

I see him, Em sent back. *You're right, he is strange.*

"Aunt Keris," Kaia said. "We're being followed."

She saw her aunt look round, and then saw her face tighten with anger.

"All right," she said. "Maybe this is someone who has done something to the inspector. We need to find somewhere quiet."

"Somewhere we can ambush him?" Em said.

Aunt Keris led the way through the streets, taking turnings, finding quieter and quieter alleys until they found one that was deserted. There was a gate there, leading into a private garden. The four of them ducked inside, waiting for the man who was following.

Kaia hadn't been able to feel a shadow in him as he followed them, but with so many people there on the street, and so far between him and them, it was possible that she simply hadn't been able to pick up on it. In the past, she'd needed to be almost on top of possessed people before she felt the shadow in them, as if it could hide deep inside them, avoiding being sensed.

"We wait here," Aunt Keris said. "And when he comes in to see where we went…"

"You ambush me?" a voice said in English.

Kaia felt a surge of fear and shock at those words, turning just in time to see the man step into the small garden space from the other side. He wasn't tall, but was thick-set, with blunt, squashed features. Those features currently held a look of contempt.

"Did you really think that you were going to deceive me that easily? I sincerely hope that your inspector is better than this, or it won't be worth having come halfway across Europe for him."

"Who are you?" Aunt Keris demanded, and as she did so, she started to reach for what Kaia assumed was a weapon.

"No, no, let's not do anything hasty," the man said, his hand coming up. He held a short-barreled revolver there, aimed steadily. "Please rest assured that I will not hesitate to shoot you if you try anything. It is not you I have been contracted to retrieve, after all."

Kaia reached out with her powers. She still couldn't sense a shadow in this man, and this close to him, she felt sure that she would be able to sense it if one of them were there in control of him.

"Contracted?" Kaia said. "What do you mean, contracted?"

"You must be Kaia," the man said. "Or is it Emmeline? No, not with that accent. Pure south of the river London, my dear. Do you know, Inspector Pinsley's superior actually believes that you have turned his head, talked him into running off with him."

Kaia made a face as she understood this man's meaning.

"Oh, I know. Hutton is *quite* mistaken," the man said. "But his money remains good, and he wants the inspector back. I believe he has a most interesting set of charges planned for him: dereliction of duty, corruption in public office... I'm sure there will be others."

"So you're another bounty hunter?" Olivia demanded. "Like the ones who tried to capture my father in Rome?"

"Oh, I'm far more than just a bounty hunter, Miss Pinsley," the man said. "I am your father's equal in every respect. His superior."

"You still haven't given us your name," Aunt Keris pointed out. Kaia could see the determination on her face. She was obviously looking for just one moment when the man in front of them wasn't paying attention, one moment in which she could strike, but there didn't seem to *be* a moment. Not when this man could pull the trigger of his gun faster than Aunt Keris could hope to close the distance between them.

"Ah, yes, forgive me. I am Mr. Frederick Illingworth, consulting detective. I undertake... delicate tasks on behalf of a number of important individuals. I find those who need to be found, bring down those who must be brought low, find answers where there are none."

"And you're here for my father?" Olivia said.

"I am. Now, tell me where he is, please."

He said it as if he were simply asking them for the correct time so that he could set his watch.

"We don't know," Kaia said. "And even if we did, we wouldn't tell you a thing."

Mr. Illingworth didn't seem impressed by her attempt at defiance. Instead, he leveled his pistol at her.

"Young lady, I don't think you understand the seriousness of your situation. You *will* tell me where the inspector is, one way or another."

"You can't make us tell you anything," Em said.

Mr. Illingworth sneered at her. "Can't I? Young lady, I have gotten answers from strong, tough men. By the time I was finished with them, they were begging to tell me everything they knew. Do you really think you're stronger than them?"

Aunt Keris moved to interpose herself. "Don't you *dare* threaten my nieces."

It just meant that Mr. Illingworth pointed the gun straight at the middle of her forehead, the threat obvious.

"I suppose I could take you all as my hostages, and use the threat of killing you one by one to draw the inspector to me," he said. "But honestly, I think you would be more trouble than you're worth. Four hostages is too many, so I will just take one."

He grabbed for Kaia, a meaty hand closing over her arm with a grip so tight that it was painful. He pulled her back from the others, all but wrenching her from her feet.

"I think the inspector will come for you, Kaia. He'd better. The others here had better tell him to, because I will hurt you, and continue to hurt you, until he does."

Kaia could see that this vile man meant the threat, and that brought a wave of fear and revulsion rising up inside her.

It brought more than that. She felt her power rising up, roaring up through her, impossible to stop. She cried out with that power, the scream bursting out of her as the power roiled out like a tidal wave. It slammed into her would-be captor then, not just breaking his grip, but lifting him off his feet and sending him flying a good ten feet through the air. He tumbled and hit the ground hard, not rising.

Aunt Keris went over to him, obviously ready to fight if he started to rise.

"He's out cold," she said, looking impressed. "Well done, Kaia."

"Maybe we should get out of here," Olivia suggested.

"Maybe we should kill him while we have the chance," Em added.

"Em!" Kaia was slightly shocked by that.

"You know he'll just hunt us down."

Aunt Keris was shaking her head, though. "No, Olivia is right. We need to leave while he's still unconscious. It will give us a chance to put some distance between us and him."

Then, once they had, they would have to start searching for the inspector again. If there was a man like this hunting for the inspector, that only meant that they needed to find him even faster.

CHAPTER FOURTEEN

Kaia and the others hurried back in the direction of the safehouse, wanting to put some distance between themselves and the man who had just tried to attack them. Kaia had to force herself to walk briskly, rather than running, knowing that trying to run would only attract attention that she and the others didn't need, making it far too easy for this "Mr. Illingworth" to track them.

"We need to watch out for the possibility that he has associates with him," Aunt Keris said, looking around as they all walked. "If I were him, I would set people out in the street, just in case we escaped."

"I don't think he planned any of this, though," Em said. "When we saw him in the square, it seemed like he'd only just noticed us."

"We still need to be careful," Aunt Keris insisted.

They needed to be careful, but that didn't mean that they could just go back to the safehouse and sit there. The shadows would be conducting their ritual tonight, and if they succeeded, then the whole world would fall to them. Kaia knew that she and her sister would have to act to stop them, even if she still had to persuade Em to take the risk of going to the Acropolis to do it.

In the meantime, though, they had a task that was at least as important, as far as Kaia was concerned.

"We need to keep looking for the inspector," she said.

"How?" Aunt Keris replied. "While I understand why you wanted to go back to the fountain, there were no new clues there, nothing that might lead us to him."

"Then we find another way," Kaia said. "The inspector wouldn't give up if it were one of us."

"We're not giving up," Olivia said. "But I'm not sure what we can do that might find him."

"What would *he* do?" Kaia countered. "He would scour the city. He would ask questions. He would try to find informants who might have seen everything."

"We don't *have* any informants in this city," Aunt Keris pointed out.

That didn't dim Kaia's determination even a little. "Then we find some. A tall Englishman wandering the streets? Someone must have seen *something*."

"She has a point," Olivia said. "And I'm not prepared to just give up on my father."

"No one is giving up," Aunt Keris said. She sighed. "All right, we'll try. You're right, Kaia: Sebastian is distinctive enough that he would be hard to miss, *especially* since that English accent of his seems to shine through no matter what language he tries to speak. If we're lucky, someone will have seen him."

She led the way down the street, looking around until she found the huddled shape of a beggar, keeping out of the sun in a doorway. It seemed to Kaia that every city had them, even ones as beautiful and quiet as this.

Aunt Keris slipped the man a couple of drachma. "We're looking for someone, a tall Englishman in a long coat. Dark hair, lean features. You'd know if you saw him."

The beggar shook his head.

"Do you know anyone who *might* have seen him?" Kaia asked.

The beggar shrugged and gestured vaguely off to another street. He still didn't say anything.

Kaia wasn't going to give up, though, and instead set off in the direction the beggar had indicated, walking along with the others until they found a stallholder selling various different meats on skewers. He looked over as they approached.

"Hello, ladies. Can I get you something?"

"We're looking for a friend of ours," Aunt Keris said, going into her description of the inspector again. She put a couple more drachma down on the stall's counter.

"I *think* I saw a man like that earlier, heading that way."

That was enough to at least set them searching, heading into what seemed to be a slightly wealthier part of town, dedicated to business. Here, unlike most of the rest of Athens, there were men dressed in formal, stuffy suits that weren't suitable for the heat. There were a couple of banks, and a large church.

They headed for a small bar that sat between them, obviously there for the refreshment of the powerful people who worked nearby. A couple of men were drinking outside.

"We're looking for our friend," Aunt Keris said. "An Englishman."

"Ah, I saw an Englishman," one of the men said, his words slightly slurred.

"Tall, with a thin face?" Olivia asked.

The man nodded, standing. "I could tell you where he is, for a kiss."

The drunk moved toward Olivia, reaching out for her. Aunt Keris was there, though, grabbing one of his wrists and twisting it painfully enough that he had to stand on tiptoes to avoid injury.

"Now, that isn't polite," she said. "I think you had better apologize, don't you?"

The drunk nodded quickly as she twisted a little more. "Sorry!"

"And the man you saw?"

"That way. *That* way!"

He pointed with his free hand. Kaia saw her aunt push him back into his chair.

"Thank you, you've been very helpful."

They continued on their way. And now it seemed that they were bouncing from hint to hint, rumor to rumor. It was obvious that most of the people they met hadn't seen the inspector, but a few, just a few, seemed to have caught glimpses of him.

It meant that they found themselves walking through the wealthy district into a space that seemed to have more people in it, all heading toward what seemed to be a large covered market. Kaia could smell the scents of food, wine, and spices coming from the place. She could hear the cries of the hawkers there trying to sell their wares, and the chatter of people as they shopped. She could see the faded paint on the marble of the place, as if it had once been richly decorated, but now had only faded white to offer the world. She saw a group of what seemed to be priests moving through the crowd on their way to somewhere else, and heard a couple of musicians playing drums and some kind of stringed instrument that looked like a guitar, only with a bowl back and no frets.

In all of it, though, there was only one thing that truly caught Kaia's eye. There, in the middle of the crowd, moving through it with a sense of purpose, was the inspector.

It was only the briefest of glimpses, but Kaia was sure it was him, striding through the crowd with that military bearing of his, so that it looked more like he was marching to battle than simply heading to a market. He stepped into the covered market, and then, in an instant, he was lost to Kaia's sight.

"There," Kaia called out, and saw the others' heads snap around. "The inspector! He went into that market!"

A sense of relief hit Kaia as she said it, because at least if the inspector was somewhere there, he was alive and safe. He hadn't been murdered by someone shadow possessed, and he hadn't been taken as a prisoner by some deadly bounty hunter. Kaia hadn't been willing to voice those fears before, because even thinking it had felt like a betrayal, but now that she could see him there, she could admit to herself that those fears had been there under the surface all along.

"Where?" Em said. "I don't see him."

"Because he went inside!" Kaia exclaimed. Obviously she wouldn't be able to see him now that he was inside.

"You're sure, Kaia?" Olivia asked. She sounded as if she hardly dared to hope that it might be true.

"I saw him," Kaia said. "I'm certain. It's not as if he exactly looks like everyone else here."

"He went inside?" Aunt Keris said. "Then we'll follow, and find out what all of this has been about. And frankly, he had better have a good explanation for it all."

Now that the prospect had come up of actually finding the inspector alive, it seemed that Aunt Keris had the space in which to finally be annoyed with the inspector for going out of the safehouse without at least trying to tell the rest of them what was going on.

Kaia wasn't quite sure *what* to think, right then. She was glad that the inspector was all right, obviously. Yet, at the same time, she also wanted to know why he hadn't come back to the safehouse. Why he'd left without saying anything. Was it because he knew that Mr. Illingworth was hunting him and he didn't want to endanger them all, or was it something else? Was this yet another of his misguided attempts to protect Kaia and the others?

The only way to find out was to catch up to him, and that meant heading into the covered market. Inside, it seemed even bigger than it had from the outside, with stall after stall set out there, selling everything from simple foodstuffs to antiques that had obviously been taken straight from the city's ruins. The air was filled with the smells of spices that simply weren't present in England, brought from the Ottoman Empire or from Africa. Meanwhile, it was barely possible to hear because so many people were talking all at once.

Kaia looked around, hoping to spot the inspector again. She thought that she caught the barest glimpse of him off to one side, talking to a stallholder, collecting a small, carefully wrapped parcel.

"There!" Kaia said, setting off in the direction she'd seen him in. It was hard, pushing her way through the crowd, but she managed to find enough gaps to slip through, going in the general direction in which she'd seen the inspector. Kaia plunged forward, while Olivia, Aunt Keris, and Em tried to keep up.

Kaia saw the inspector again, adjusted her course through the crowd, and kept going. It was impossible to keep him in sight when everyone was taller than her, but she could use the glimpses she got of him to keep moving forward, trying to get closer.

He was there, ahead, standing at a stall that contained a grinding wheel, there to sharpen knives. The inspector seemed to be talking something over with the owner, who took a knife from him and started to work on it.

Kaia made her way forward, determined to catch up to the inspector before he moved on.

"Inspector!" she called out as she got closer. "Inspector, it's me, Kaia!"

He didn't react, didn't seem to have heard her above the crowd, so Kaia called out again as she neared him.

"It's Kaia!" she called. "Where have you been, Inspector?"

Inspector Pinsley turned toward her then, and there was a strange, almost rictus smile on his face that Kaia had never seen from him before. She saw it, and a second later, she felt a deep sense of wrongness, of something at odds with the world, that hated it.

"No," Kaia said, not willing to believe that the feeling was coming from the inspector. Just the thought of it made her skin crawl, made her want to deny the possibility of it with every fiber of her being. Yet every step closer made the feeling grow stronger, made it impossible to deny that it was coming from within Inspector Pinsley.

Deep horror filled Kaia then, because she knew what that sensation meant. Kaia had felt it before when close to people, and each of those people had turned out to be dangerous, turned out to be a killer, or a potential killer. It was a feeling that meant only one thing, and just the thought of what it meant made tears rise in the corners of Kaia's eyes. She knew then why the inspector had left:

He had been possessed by a shadow.

CHAPTER FIFTEEN

The shadow that was Inspector Sebastian Pinsley was quite pleased with its upgrade in host. The girl Cassiopeia had been a useful vessel for the early stages of all of this, and an amusing way to sample all of the pleasures of the human world, but there was something about the inspector that was far more suited to these last hours.

For one thing, he was a man of the right kind of age, and that made some things simply easier in a world where people equated those things with authority. He found that no one questioned him now. No one tried to explain to him all the ways in which his ideas would not work, or questioned whether he really meant what he said.

Then there was the fact that he was simply larger and stronger than he had been. It was easy for a shadow to unlock the full potential of a body's muscles, granting strength beyond that of most humans, but that potential was still limited by size, and by the existing power of the muscles the host possessed. Pinsley gave the shadow much more potential when it came to violent acts.

Even the mind was helpful. While the host's consciousness was locked away behind walls of the shadow's devising, it was still useful to have access to resources of memory and analysis, deduction and existing knowledge. Inspector Pinsley was a treasure trove in that regard, which made the shadow grateful that it had decided to take him, rather than attempting to kill him with the body it possessed before. The upgrade would make its plans go much smoother.

They were *its* plans. In so far as the shadows had leaders, it was one, or at least, it was more powerful than the others of its kind, and that amounted to the same thing. It had no name, nor badge of office, nor title; such things were for the hateful human world of form and order. Still those other shadows that brushed against it knew its power and hastened to obey, because they did not want to suffer its violence.

Those plans would allow for the destruction of the human world, for its capture, for its conquest. If you could call it a conquest. The simple fact was that, once the great portal was opened, it would be about the possession and replacement of the human race, not commanding them through threats of violence, the way they did with one another.

They would take the world of form and order, tearing down its structures, remaking it in their images. Perhaps others of its kind would want to destroy things completely, but the shadow had seen more of this world now, had come to understand all the ways that having a physical form could be better and more pleasurable than the alternative. No, rather than destroying it, the shadows would take it. They would claim the humans as their own, farm them, control them like cattle, and walk among them like gods.

All thanks to the inspector, and the moment when the shadow had decided not to kill him.

*

The shadow that was Cassiopeia crouched outside the shadowseers' safehouse in the darkness before the dawn, watching for movement, trying to get a sense of who was there. Once it was sure that most of those there were asleep, it crept forward to the door. That was locked, and there were runes there that were designed to try to deter its kind.

Perhaps on the least of them, on those untethered from a body, they might even have worked. Cassiopeia, though, found it easy to obscure them long enough to start to work on the lock. This body had spent some time as a petty thief, and its hands knew the workings of a lock. It took only minutes to open, letting Cassiopeia inside in silence.

It was dark in the entrance hall, but darkness was not an obstacle. She could see light in a dining room: a candle that flickered. Even now that the shadow had been a part of her for a while, it took a moment or two to remind herself that it was no threat to her. She crept forward instead, moving quietly.

There was a young man in the dining room, seated at the table, his fingers drumming against it, obviously too agitated to sleep. But then, he had a right to be agitated. After all, he had been there when Cassiopeia had brought about the ambush that killed his friends. He had seen that there was a power hunting for him that would not be satisfied until he was dead.

His back was to the door, and that let Cassiopeia creep forward, drawing a slender blade.

Please, please no. There must be another way, O Goddess...

The voice of the host was irritating. The foolish girl seemed to think that the shadow was a god or goddess inhabiting her body. She certainly seemed to react poorly to some of the things the shadow had wanted to do while it had her form, screaming inside when Cassiopeia

83

had experimented a little with torturing others, or explored the more intricate pleasures of the addict.

The shadow ignored her now, moving forward, deflecting the shadows she cast so that they would not be visible to the young man as she neared him. Even then, something must have alerted him to her presence. He turned toward her, eyes wide with terror.

"You!"

"Did you think you could get away from me so easily?" Cassiopeia asked.

The shadowseer's mouth opened, to answer or to call for help, Cassiopeia didn't know. She didn't give him enough time for either, bringing the knife she held around instead, slicing across his throat with wicked speed. Cassiopeia clutched him close then, watching him die, not caring that blood stained her forearms. All that mattered was that the last shadowseer in the city was dead.

Except...

Except that Cassiopeia could feel some hint of their strange talent elsewhere in the house, even now. Were there more? Had there been members of their kind left behind there? Or was this some new group, there to investigate because of what had happened? When one of them had escaped, the danger was always that they would manage to get news out about it all.

Still, Cassiopeia could deal with all of that. One shadowseer or a dozen, it made no difference to her. She could kill as many as she needed to.

Cassiopeia made her way upstairs. She guessed that the others would be asleep then, so it took little effort for her to sneak there silently, pushing open the door to one of the bedrooms. She saw two girls sleeping there, both around fifteen. Cassiopeia could feel the power there, far greater than that of any normal shadowseer. Cassiopeia was growing more used to the nuances of human features, too, and could see that these looked almost identical.

Shadowseer twins, just like out of the legends.

Cassiopeia thought for a few moments, fingering the edge of her blade. It would be so easy to sneak over and cut their throats while they slept. Yet she backed away instead. Two such as this made things *far* more interesting. Instead, she crept back downstairs, heading for the front door.

She was almost there when a tall, middle-aged man came out into her path. Cassiopeia shoved him aside on instinct and sprang for the door. It wasn't that she was scared of *him*, but she didn't want to risk being caught up in a fight long enough that those twins could get involved. She ran instead, heading down the street.

She heard the sound of his footsteps following her.

"Stop right there!"

Cassiopeia didn't stop, but instead ducked around a corner, and then wove shadows around herself. She waited for the man to come around the corner, and then moved behind him smoothly, setting her knife to his throat.

It would have been easy in that moment to cut his throat, but something made Cassiopeia hesitate. Possibilities came to her, questions to which she needed answers.

"You know the twins from the house, yes?" she said.

"If you harm them…" the man began, anger suffusing his voice.

"Ah, know them, *and* care for them. As I imagine they may care for you."

"I will tell you nothing."

He sounded determined. People generally did, when they still thought they had a choice about anything.

"I tire of this vessel," she said, knowing that anyone in a shadowseer place would know what she meant. "I have need of another. I think I will try you."

"Try if you want," the man said.

He had the confidence of one who knew that his will would drive her out. Still, Cassiopeia could think of ways to make him hers.

"You will let me be a part of you," she said. "Imagine the power I could give you."

"I am not interested in your promises," the man snapped back.

"No? Not even when the alternative is that I cut your throat?"

Even that didn't get a fear reaction from him. This one was brave, as well as strong. Good.

"I will not let you in," he said.

"Oh, you will," Cassiopeia said. "But if threats to yourself won't do it, how about this? After I kill you, I will go back to the shadowseer house, and I will cut the throats of everyone there while they sleep. Do you care about *them*, human?"

"Leave them out of this!" he snarled.

"That is your choice," Cassiopeia said. "Consider this: when we are joined, there will still be a part of you in me. You *might* be able to stop me from doing such a thing."

She gave that a few seconds to sink in, hearing the man's breathing accelerate as he made his decision, seeing his hands ball into fists.

"Very well," he said at last. "But you leave them alone."

"Of course," the shadow said, and then poured out of Cassiopeia's mouth, straight into that of the waiting man. It filled him, became him, and almost casually, it shoved Cassiopeia aside, setting off through Athens.

*

The shadow that was Pinsley was still considering how it had come to be him when he realized that someone was approaching him through the market. *Several* people, in fact, converging on his position through the crowd at speed.

"Inspector!"

He heard Kaia's voice before he turned toward her. The shadow knew her name now, thanks to Pinsley's memories. It knew all that she and the inspector had been through together, solving murders and hunting shadows in London, Paris, Munich, and Rome. It knew her power, both because it could feel it and because the inspector's memories showed it exactly what Kaia could do.

She was powerful indeed. So powerful that a part of the shadow wondered if it should have tried to cut her throat while it had the chance.

Instead, it turned toward the girl and smiled.

"Hello, Kaia."

"You aren't the inspector," she said, as if that were a simple fact.

"Oh, I am," the shadow said. "I am him, and so much more. Such a fine mind he has, so neat, so ordered. Everything that my kind should hate. Except that he is useful. So very useful."

"I'm going to give you one chance to leave him," Kaia warned. She started to raise her hand, as if it were a weapon she was bringing to bear. The shadow supposed that it was, in its way. Certainly those powers of hers might be inconvenient.

It had weapons of its own, of course. The inspector's revolver sat in its usual pocket, and now the shadow reached for it, dragging it out in one smooth movement, pointing it at Kaia.

Then it pointed it straight up, firing it twice into the air.

As people screamed and milled around in an effort to get away, the shadow ran.

CHAPTER SIXTEEN

Kaia flinched as the inspector fired into the air, sending the people in the covered market into tumultuous chaos, all of them trying to get away at once. In that chaos, he disappeared, slipping behind a stall and moving into the crowd.

"What's going on, Kaia?" Olivia demanded. "Why would my father do something like that?"

"He's possessed!" Kaia yelled over the cries of the crowd. "A shadow is inside him!"

She could see the look of horror on Olivia's face. It mirrored how Kaia felt right then. The inspector meant so much to her, and now a shadow had control of him, could force his body to do anything. It could make him walk out into the street and start killing people, so that everyone would believe he was a murderer.

Only the blood on Cassiopeia's hands when they'd found her told Kaia that the inspector wasn't already. The shadow had obviously forced the girl to kill Nasos before it took the inspector, and there was a kind of relief in that. Kaia didn't want the inspector to have to live with being made to do something like that.

"He's getting away," Aunt Keris said. "We can still drive the shadow out of him if we can catch him, but to do that, we have to find him."

Her aunt had a point. There was no time to lose, if they were going to catch up to the inspector. Kaia set off into the crowd, heading in the direction that she thought Inspector Pinsley had gone in, looking out for any sign of him. He might be trying to hide and escape now, but he was still taller than almost anyone else there in the market, and wearing a coat that would help to mark him out from everyone else there.

Kaia thought she saw a brief flicker of that coat somewhere ahead, near a stall that sold rugs that looked as though they'd been brought from far further off than Greece. Kaia ran for that stall, trying to get there before the inspector could get too far away.

That wasn't easy. Kaia had thought that getting through the crowds in the street was difficult, but at least they had all been moving fairly normally. Here, there were people pushing and running, some trying desperately to get away, others trying to get closer to the source of the shots, as if they simply wanted a good view of whatever was going on.

It meant that Kaia found herself pushed from every side, and had to shove back simply to make any progress. Someone lurched into her from the side, and Kaia found herself falling, having to cover her head with her hands just so that she wouldn't be trampled.

Em was there then, grabbing her arm and pulling Kaia to her feet.

"Can you see him?" Kaia shouted above the din of people trying to get away.

"That way, I think!" Em said, pointing toward a series of stalls where meat hung on hooks, waiting to be sold or carved.

Kaia looked around, trying to see her aunt and Olivia. They were there in the crowd, pushing their way through, but there was no time to wait for them. She and Em had to get to the inspector if they were going to drive the shadow out of him and save him.

They ran for the food stalls, picking their way through the crowd. As they got closer, Kaia thought she saw the inspector for another brief moment, ducking in between those hanging sides of meat. Kaia ran after him, able to move a little more freely in this part of the hall.

She was moving so quickly that she barely had enough time to jump out of the way as a metal hook came swinging at her, passing by Kaia close enough that she could feel it. She dodged to the side, feeling a sudden burst of fear as a whole side of beef came swinging at her, set in motion by Inspector Pinsley shoving it. She couldn't avoid it completely, and the sheer weight of it sent her stumbling.

That gave the inspector enough time to run again, even as Kaia tried to raise a hand to bring her powers to bear.

"Not here!" Aunt Keris said, catching up to her. "There are too many people who might be hurt. We just have to keep following him."

Kaia set off again through the crowds of the covered market, and now she could see the inspector making progress of his own, heading for one side of the place. Kaia could see a door there, and she realized that the inspector was trying to escape into the streets of Athens, attempting to put some distance between them as he fled.

Kaia ran for that door, determined to keep as close to him as she could, while Em, Aunt Keris, and Olivia kept pace.

She saw the inspector burst out into the street, but it was only moments later when Kaia followed him, blinking in the sudden sunlight. She saw a tall figure running away to her left, knew it had to be the inspector, and set off in pursuit.

Even as she did so, the inspector turned, his gun raised in his hand once again. This time, he didn't fire upwards. Instead, he shot at their small group, sending fragments flying from the wall of a house near Kaia. She kept running forward, and the shots kept coming, but none of them got close to her. Kaia wanted to believe that meant that the inspector was still in there somewhere, jerking the hand that held the gun so that the bullets went wide. Honestly, though, it might just have been because the inspector wasn't any better a shot with a shadow in him than without.

Either way, the shots bought the inspector more time in which to run, because Kaia and the others had to duck out of the way each time he fired. It meant that he had enough time to dart around a corner, forcing them to chase him into the back alleys of Athens.

Kaia sprinted after him, hoping that she wasn't going to turn a corner only to walk into the barrel of a gun. She skidded around the corner, saw the inspector darting into another side street, and followed.

"Keep up!" Olivia said, running quickly after her father. "We can't lose him. We can't let that *thing* have him!"

Kaia could hear the determination there, and the fear. After all, she had only just found her father again after years of being apart following her mother's murder.

The four of them followed, taking quick turnings, trying to catch up to the inspector. He had all the speed and strength that came from being a shadow, though, plus the simple advantage of height and long legs to carry him away faster. Kaia started to suspect that they would never catch up to him if he kept running like this.

They had to try, though, and not just to save the inspector. It was obvious that this shadow was central to the plans the others had at the Acropolis. It had been the one trying to work out plans in the house Cassiopeia had taken. It had been the one drawing designs for something relating to the portal. If Kaia could get to it, rip it out of the inspector, and destroy it, that might slow down the shadows' plans and stop them from opening their great portal tonight.

That thought filled Kaia with hope as she ran around the next corner, and she felt even better as she realized that it was a dead end. The shadow had taken a wrong turn, and now its back was to a wall as it tried to work out what to do next.

It raised the inspector's pistol, and a fresh wave of fear filled Kaia. At this range, she suspected that even the inspector couldn't miss. Would he do it? Would he actually…

The inspector pulled the trigger, and Kaia heard the gun click empty.

There was no time in which to focus on the relief that flooded her then, because the inspector was already moving to reload. Kaia and the others charged forward in that second or two, moving to grab him.

Dropping his gun, the inspector fought back.

He would have been a dangerous opponent even without a shadow in him. The inspector was a former soldier who seemed to know all about pugilism and wrestling, and who had weight and size on his side. The presence of the shadow in him only made him more dangerous. As Aunt Keris closed in, he hit out at her with a jab and a cross, then sidestepped suddenly, slamming his shoulder into Olivia to send her sprawling.

As she started to rise, the inspector spun toward Kaia, throwing a punch her way that she barely dodged in time.

"Grab him!" Aunt Keris shouted. "Our only hope is to grab him all at once!"

Kaia nodded and lunged forward at the inspector. He threw her off as easily as he might have flung aside a small child, so that Kaia had a moment when she was airborne, and only just remembered to roll when she hit the floor. She came up, her head spinning, and threw herself forward again.

This time, she managed to latch onto one of the inspector's legs. He lifted a hand to strike her, but Aunt Keris was there then, intercepting the blow and wrenching the arm into a lock to force the inspector to the floor. Em and Olivia jumped on him, adding their weight to the attempt to hold Inspector Pinsley down. Even then, it was hard work, because he fought and thrashed, obviously determined to throw them off even if it hurt him in the process. The shadow wouldn't care about that; it could always steal another body.

Kaia reached down for her power then, determined to drive the thing out. The worry she felt for the inspector made it easy to find that power, easy to call it up through her and project it out, light pouring into Inspector Pinsley in an effort to leave nowhere within him for the shadow to hide. Kaia threw power at him, determined to burn the shadow out, readying herself for the moment when it would issue from his mouth and nose, and when she would be able to try to destroy it in the open air.

It *didn't* leave the inspector, though. Instead, he continued to thrash and fight, an arm breaking free so that he got a hand around Olivia's throat and squeezed. It was getting harder to hold onto him by the moment.

Aunt Keris seemed to realize that as well, because she chose that moment to rear up over the inspector, relaxing her grip for a moment as she pulled her arm back.

"Apologies, Sebastian, but this is for your own good."

She swung a punch forward that connected sweetly with the inspector's jaw in the sound of bone hitting bone. The inspector slumped back into unconsciousness, and even as he did so, Kaia saw her aunt searching his pockets, coming out with the set of handcuffs that he kept there.

"I couldn't get the shadow out of him," Kaia said. "That's never happened before."

The thought that she might not be able to get the shadow out of the inspector made Kaia feel sick with worry. The inspector was like a father to her. She had to be able to free him from its control. She had to.

"It may just have been the stress of the fight," Aunt Keris said. "It doesn't matter now. What matters is that we need to restrain him and get him back to the shadowseers' safehouse. Once we have him there, we can take our time about exorcising this shadow properly."

CHAPTER SEVENTEEN

Mr. Illingworth woke slowly, with a headache that was only compounded by the piercing light of the Greek sun. He wasn't sure how long he'd been unconscious at first, but the fractional movement of the sun across the sky gave him at least a rough idea, and his pocket watch confirmed it. Almost half an hour.

What had hit him hard enough to achieve *that*?

Mr. Illingworth scoured his memories for an answer to that question, but the things he remembered didn't make a great deal of sense. His memory insisted that a young woman had put out her hand, screamed like some kind of banshee, and flung him across the space of the courtyard garden without ever having to touch him.

Such a thing was clearly impossible, the kind of thing that Illingworth would have dismissed as a particularly poor piece of theater if he had seen it at a fairground or acted out upon the street. It was the kind of thing a stage magician might do, except that it wouldn't be very convincing to the audience, because it would be only too obvious that the individual being thrown was playing along.

Except that Mr. Illingworth *hadn't* played along. He had been fully intending violence, and somehow a girl half his size had sent him flying.

That was a conundrum, and one that Mr. Illingworth wanted to solve. He wanted to reassure himself that the world remained as orderly and as neat as he knew it to be, a place that he could deconstruct with logic, turning it to his advantage in all the ways that he'd spent years perfecting.

So he started to go around the small square of the garden, looking for any signs of anything that might have made the effect possible. There were no hidden pulleys that he could see, nothing that someone could surreptitiously have attached him to while the girl served as a distraction, letting a team of strong men yank him backwards off his feet. In any case, such a thing would rely on him being in a particular, predetermined spot, and that seemed implausible given that he had been following Kaia and her companions through the streets, and that they had not known beforehand that he would be doing so.

92

No, that explanation was unlikely. Alternatives, then? Mr. Illingworth checked himself over carefully, looking for any sign that he might have been drugged, and that this was all a delusion brought on by some foreign substance introduced to his system. He knew the signs of such things well, however, having slipped more than a few suspects sedatives in his time, and could find no evidence that it had been done to him. Nor were there any injuries that might indicate, for example, a shotgun loaded with rock salt, fired at close range.

A shotgun? The idea that he wouldn't have heard a shotgun was a patent impossibility. The only problem was that Mr. Illingworth was running out of ideas, and the more he looked at this problem…

…well, the more it looked as though this girl might *actually* have flung him away with some kind of invisible force.

Mr. Illingworth wanted to say that such a thing was impossible, but he was a man of reason. *Truly* a man of reason. He didn't cling to what he believed to be true out of some kind of dogma, didn't fall prey to the stories that other people might try to tell themselves to explain away what they had seen. When the facts changed, he changed with them. It was the only way to survive in the shadowy facets of the world he occupied.

Right now, Mr. Illingworth's mind was changing in a way that he would have deemed impossible just a few hours ago. He felt it opening to a new possibility like a flower turning toward the light of the sun, and, just as he would have a flower, Mr. Illingworth started to pick that possibility apart with the greatest care as he started to walk back through the streets of Athens, heading for the small café where the owner had served him orange cake. It seemed as good a place as any to consider the possibility that there might actually be… Illingworth tried to think of a better word than "magic" and failed.

He returned to the café, bought more coffee, and sat there contemplating the uncanny. His men in Rome had said that the girls with the inspector could do impossible things, that they had sent the two of them flying. At the time, Mr. Illingworth had been convinced that they were lying to cover up their incompetence or disloyalty. Now, it seemed strangely possible that they had been doing no more than telling the simple, unvarnished truth.

The only question now was what that meant.

Mr. Illingworth took out his ledger and his fountain pen, wanting to make notes on all of this. At the top of a page, he wrote *Hypothesis: Magic Exists.*

He carefully wrote down the evidence of his own experience, and that of his two subordinates. He steepled his fingers as he considered the implications. If there was magic in the world, did that invalidate logical thinking? No. It merely meant that he had possessed insufficient information to date about what was really out there in the world.

Might a man of his talents be able to make use of magic?

That was an obvious second question. Mr. Illingworth suspected that there were two possibilities here: either such forces were a talent like an ear for music, or they were a series of learned skills. The raw, intuitive way in which the girl Kaia had lashed out at him suggested that there was a strong component of the former, yet Mr. Illingworth had certainly heard of groups who gave themselves over to the pursuit of otherworldly knowledge, so perhaps there was a learned component as well.

A small piece of information nagged at the back of Mr. Illingworth's brain, and he found himself sorting through his leather-bound ledger until he found what he was looking for. When he did, he stared down at the page, possibilities arranging and rearranging themselves in his mind.

Baron Vogler, the Bavarian nobleman Pinsley and the others had stayed with on their journey, had been a noted collector of purported arcana, and had gathered around him a group of what Mr. Illingworth had offhandedly assumed were fraudulent psychics and deluded would-be magicians.

Yet, what if they weren't deluded? Proceeding from the possibility that magic was real, might it not also be possible to suggest that the baron's little group might have some access to it, and that the objects he collected might have powers beyond ordinary mortal ken?

Mr. Illingworth found himself considering the journey that Pinsley and the girl Kaia had taken in a significantly different light in that moment. Previously, it had seemed like a madcap, illogical journey that suggested that one or both of them had become deranged at some point.

Now though, Mr. Illingworth started to see deeper patterns. Was it possible that Pinsley had come across the uncanny in London in some form, and that it had drawn him to the girl? From what Mr. Illingworth understood, their earliest escapade together had involved individuals who had babbled about shadows killing people, and who had claimed that there were forces of darkness in the world behind everything.

At the time, those individuals had quite rightly been dismissed as mad, but what if they weren't? Was it possible that Kaia had shown the inspector this shadow world, this demi-monde, while they were both in London?

If so, what effect would it have had on the inspector? He was a man of logic, much like Mr. Illingworth, so it was hard to believe that the effect would be anything other than significant. Being shown a world like that would have demanded an extreme reaction; it could not just be ignored.

The journey to Paris made sense because of the family connections they both possessed there, although the chaos that ensued suggested to Mr. Illingworth that there had been something of that shadow world in the city.

Munich now made sense. They had gone there to learn more or… no, they had been seeking some kind of item from the Baron's collection. And they had not found it, because Mr. Illingworth's notes suggested that their little group had split up, searching in both Venice and Rome. Now they were in Athens, a place of myth and legend, and there had to be a reason for that.

Mr. Illingworth found himself going over his other notes, the ones about government ministers, secrets, and hints, things that he thought ran the world. He found himself scribbling furiously in the margins, trying to work out if any of *this* side of things might have been affected by the shadow world. Was the former Home Secretary who claimed he had no memory of how he had come to be caught in a compromising position with an actress telling the truth? Had a unit of sappers who had disappeared in the Raj merely deserted, or was something more uncanny going on?

Mr. Illingworth saw the possibilities in all of it. A man with access to such powers might be able to learn secrets that no spy could fathom. He might wield power and influence on levels that people could not comprehend, and so could not hope to counter. He might become something far *more* than Mr. Illingworth had ever conceived of being.

He found himself standing and going over to the café owner, forcing a smile that he suspected the woman would appreciate.

"The last time I was here," he said, "I asked you about strange goings-on in the city."

"And I told you, there have been all kinds of noises in the night, and strangers. There have been people behaving oddly, just walking out of their homes or changing their personality overnight."

Ordinarily, Mr. Illingworth would have suspected some kind of blackmail in those circumstances, but now, he was beginning to contemplate the possibility that some kind of magical control might be involved. Amazing, really, how quickly and completely one's mind could change on such things.

"And have there been any particular places where people have been behaving strangely?" he asked.

"Well, I suppose there are a lot of people up at the Acropolis at the moment," the café owner said. "I assumed it was just kids, but people say there are all sorts up there, behaving oddly. Someone should do something."

If Mr. Illingworth was correct in his assumptions, someone was planning to. Pinsley and the girl had crossed Europe, delving into some kind of uncanny business, and now, he suspected, the Acropolis was where the next part of it would unfold.

Mr. Illingworth intended to be there for two reasons. First, he intended to kill or capture Sebastian Pinsley. That was his contract, and he always fulfilled his contracts, magic or not.

Secondly, he wanted the girl and her sister. With what she had done to him, it seemed obvious that she was his path to gaining control of magic, and magic, Mr. Illingworth suspected, would give him all the power he could have ever dreamed of.

So he would follow them, and when they came to the Acropolis, he would be ready.

CHAPTER EIGHTEEN

Kaia struggled to contain her feelings as she stood in front of the inspector. He was currently tied to a chair in a bedroom of the safehouse, light streaming down at him from several windows. With a shadow, they needed as much light as they could get to keep that shadow from escaping.

Not that there was much. It had taken so long to get the inspector back there through the streets that the light was fading to the deep red of sunset. Already they'd set out candles around the inspector, wanting to make sure that they had enough light to contain him.

The others were in there too, Olivia looking on with obvious worry, Aunt Keris looking as though she was trying to work through the situation in her head, Em looking like she just wanted to do something. Kaia was just looking at the inspector, hoping that everything was going to be all right.

"If you're looking for your inspector in here, don't bother," the shadow said with Pinsley's mouth. "I have him solidly shut away. He won't help you."

"We'll get him back soon enough," Aunt Keris said. "For the moment, I thought it might be useful to talk with you."

Kaia looked over to her aunt, not happy with this idea at all. "You want to interrogate the shadow? I thought we brought the inspector here to exorcise it."

"We did," her aunt agreed. "But this is a chance to learn more about what the shadows are doing, and the best ways to disrupt their plans."

"And in the meantime, my father is possessed by that *thing*?" Olivia demanded, obviously not liking the idea any more than Kaia did.

"If he were here, I believe Sebastian would understand," Aunt Keris said. "He is a practical man. He would see the need for more information."

The shadow laughed then. "And you think you're going to get it from me? What are you going to do? Cut strips from my flesh? Stick hot needles under my fingernails? Having done both to people, I can assure you that they cause the most *exquisite* pain. But I don't think you'll want to do that to your dear inspector, will you?"

Just the thought of anything like that made Kaia feel sick. She couldn't stand seeing the inspector possessed like this. She wasn't *going* to stand for it. Reaching for her power, she flung it into the inspector, determined to drive the shadow out of him. The power flooded through him, rising up, trying to leave no place for the shadow to go within him.

Kaia saw the inspector's hands clutching the side of the chair hard, saw his face set with tension, but still the shadow didn't leave him.

Then Aunt Keris was grabbing her arm, pulling Kaia back. "Stop, Kaia! I know you want Sebastian to be safe. I do too, but we need all the information we can get if we are to stop everything the shadows have planned tonight."

"You're not going to get anything," the shadow said, sitting there as calmly as if nothing had just happened, as if Kaia hadn't just tried to push it out of the inspector's body. "And as for forcing me out of this one... I am far too powerful for that, girl. I am not some weakling to be shredded by your light. I am the strongest of my kind. I am the dark itself."

"You see," Aunt Keris said, "we're learning things already. I wonder if the others of you will want you back. If they *need* you back for this ritual of theirs."

"The world will change, if I am there or not," the shadow said. "There is nothing you can do to stop it."

"I think you're lying," Aunt Keris said. "I think that you wouldn't be here in the city if you didn't have a role to play in all of this. You wouldn't have taken over a human if you didn't have things to do in the human world."

"Or perhaps I have just decided that I like having that kind of control," the shadow countered, with a smile. Kaia had the feeling that it was enjoying playing this game with her aunt, never quite giving her anything, never quite admitting anything. "When this ritual is complete, my kind shall be as gods among you. It will let us into the world with the power to take over anyone, not just those who are already weak or corrupt. We will float among you, claiming those we require, doing as we wish with the rest."

The fact that it was willing to say that much suggested to Kaia that it was confident there was nothing any of them could do to stop it. Or maybe that was just what the shadow wanted them to think. She still had the relic. She'd closed portals before, and destroyed shadows. The ritual of the shadowseers might be too dangerous, but she could still do plenty.

98

"I think if it were that easy," Aunt Keris said, "you wouldn't have spent so much time in the city. You wouldn't have so carefully hunted down the shadowseers."

"You don't know what you're talking about," the inspector said. It was easy to remember that it wasn't really him, because Inspector Pinsley never normally sneered at people like that, or had that harsh note in his voice.

"I think I do," Aunt Keris said. "I saw the things you wrote on the chalkboards when you were Cassiopeia, the ways you sought to understand the ritual."

"As if your mind could comprehend any of it," the shadow said.

"I saw the spot where something was missing," Aunt Keris said, sounding triumphant as she taunted the shadow. "I saw that you don't have all you need to finish this. You aren't going to succeed, are you?"

Now the shadow strained against its bonds, anger staining the inspector's face. "I'll take my time when I kill you," he snarled. "I'll make you beg for death before it comes!"

Just the vehemence with which he said that told Kaia that her aunt had hit on something. Was it true? Did the shadows really not have whatever final piece they needed to finish the ritual? Was the world safe?

Or was this all a bluff to stop Kaia and the others from interfering?

"I think we have what we need," Aunt Keris said. She looked around at Kaia and Em. "*Now* it's time to get the inspector back."

Kaia nodded. It had been hard to hold back from doing this before. Now, she wasn't going to hesitate. She took out the relic and immediately saw the way the inspector's eyes followed it.

"It's this, isn't it?" she said. "This is the missing piece."

The inspector said nothing, but Kaia was sure that it was true. Why else would Prince Raoul have been searching for it in Munich, or the shadows in Rome be trying to find it? Kaia had thought that it was just to stop the shadowseers getting it to stop their plans, but with all of this… it made sense that it would be the missing piece. It was a central part of the shadowseers' ritual, and that was what the shadows were trying to pervert now to their own ends.

If they kept the relic safe, the shadows wouldn't be able to complete their version of the ritual.

For now, though, the only part that mattered was getting the shadow out of the inspector. Kaia was a little surprised by just how much she needed that, needed him to be safe. He'd been like a father to her, and the thought of losing him filled her with terror.

She reached out the hand with the orb to Em, and Em put her hand over Kaia's. Their powers rose in response to the contact.

"Leave willingly, and you at least have a chance to run," Aunt Keris said. "I have seen Kaia shred your kind to nothingness before.

The inspector laughed then, and that laugh was too much for Kaia. She lashed out with all the power she and Em had, throwing it into the inspector, shoving every scrap of power she could muster into him in an effort to force the shadow out.

The inspector gritted his teeth as the power flooded through him. His hands tightened on the chair until his knuckles went white. Then he screamed, a great roar of pain and anger that sent shivers through Kaia.

Still the shadow didn't leave him.

Kaia sent more power into him, and she saw blood trickling from the inspector's nose. She heard the sounds of pain he made, and a terrifying thought filled her. What if the shadow was twined so tightly around his being that ripping it away from him was hurting him, even killing him? What if the shadow had sent roots deep into him, so that pulling it away would leave great gaping wounds in the inspector that he couldn't survive?

Just the thought of that made Kaia pull back, stopping before she hurt the inspector more.

"Is that all you have?" the inspector asked, in a mocking tone.

"I'll show you what we have!" Em said, starting toward him, her power rising again.

Kaia caught her sister, pulling her back. "What are you doing?"

"I'm doing what's needed to get that thing out of him," Em snapped. "What are *you* doing, Kaia? Why did you stop?"

"It was hurting the inspector!"

"That's what the shadow wants you to think. He can take it."

"And if he can't?" Kaia demanded. "What then?"

Aunt Keris stepped between them. "Outside, girls. Both of you. Now."

Reluctantly, Kaia went out of the room with Em, her aunt, and Olivia. They shut the door behind them, because the last thing Kaia wanted right then was for the shadow to see them arguing.

"It isn't doing any good arguing among ourselves," Aunt Keris said. "It won't help to get the shadow out of the inspector."

"Why are you telling me?" Em shot back. "I'm not the one who was holding back."

"I wasn't holding back," Kaia insisted. At least, she didn't think she had been.

100

"Of course you were," Em said. "You were so worried about hurting the inspector that you won't do what you have to do to *save* him. That's the difference between us, Kaia. You might be the one with all the power but I'm the one who does what's needed."

Was that jealousy Kaia heard in her sister's voice?

"I didn't choose to be more powerful than you, Em," Kaia said.

"No, but Aunt Keris chose to give you the relic on top of all that power," Em replied. Had she been upset about this ever since Rome? Kaia had thought they'd solved it. "Yet here, you won't even use that power to save the inspector."

"That's enough," Olivia said. "Both of you. That's enough. My father is the one in danger here, and yet you're squabbling like you're both half as old as you are. I know you're both worried about him, about this whole situation, but that's no reason to—"

Olivia broke off as a crash of splintering wood came from the room beyond the door. A moment later, Kaia heard the sound of breaking glass.

"No," Kaia said, realizing what was happening.

She ran back into the room just in time to see Inspector Pinsley poised on the edge of the window.

"I'll see you at the Acropolis," he said, and then dove out of the window, onto the street below. He rolled as he hit, then came up running. Kaia made to lunge after him, but her aunt grabbed her.

"You'd break a leg at least. Come on, down the stairs."

They ran down there, but it took almost a minute to reach the front door and get it open. By that time, the inspector was gone. Kaia thought she could feel the presence of the shadow, but even that gave her only a general direction, and it was fading quickly.

The shadow in the inspector was free again, the shadows were still up there at the Acropolis, and it was getting dark. They might be just hours away from the shadows' portal opening. They had to get to the Acropolis.

CHAPTER NINETEEN

"What do you mean, we're not going?" Kaia asked her aunt, staring at her in disbelief at the door of the safehouse.

"I mean exactly that," Aunt Keris said. "The best thing for us to do right now is to go nowhere near the Acropolis."

That made no sense to Kaia. "But that's where the inspector is going to *be*. That's where the shadows are planning to open their portal. That's where—"

"That's where they have obviously laid some kind of trap for us," Aunt Keris said. "The shadow's last words to us were to tell us where he was going to be. Why would he say that if not to lure us in?"

Kaia couldn't believe that her aunt was being so reluctant about all of this. "I thought you were the one who wanted us to go to the Acropolis to stop the shadows before."

"Yes," Aunt Keris agreed. "But that *was* before, not now. Come back inside, all of you."

She led them back into the safehouse, and Kaia's first instinct was to turn and run after the inspector. Olivia and Em seemed to have anticipated that, though, making sure that Kaia went in ahead of them.

Aunt Keris led the way through to the dining room of the safehouse. There was no trace now of the murder that had taken place there, while Casper and Cassiopeia were away in the drawing room. It seemed that the young shadowseer was taking his role as a protector for the young woman seriously.

Aunt Keris sat on one side of the table, her hands on it, as if waiting for Kaia to throw an angry outburst her way. Kaia had to force herself to speak more calmly. She wasn't going to give her aunt the satisfaction of making her look like some child having a tantrum.

"Why have you changed your mind?" Kaia asked. "Why do you suddenly want to abandon the inspector?"

"I don't *want* to do any such thing," Aunt Keris said. "But I believe that we have no choice. As a shadowseer, my task is to protect humanity from the shadows."

"So we should be up there fighting them," Kaia insisted.

Her aunt shook her head. "No. That is precisely what we must not do, in this instance."

Kaia looked around at the others, to try to see if they understood any of Aunt Keris's strangely back to front reasoning.

"Because of the relic?" Olivia said. Apparently she *did* understand it, and that seemed impossibly strange to Kaia when it had been her father who had just walked out of there, possessed by a shadow.

Aunt Keris nodded. "Exactly. The shadows require a missing component to finish their ritual. I believe that component to be the relic. If we walk up there with it to take them on, then, should we lose, we are as good as handing them the very thing they need to take control of the world."

"We won't lose," Kaia insisted. She looked to Em for support. "Tell them, Em. We're not frightened just because there will be shadows there."

Em was always eager for a fight, always the first to leap into the action. For what had to be the first time since she'd met her, though, Kaia saw her sister hesitate.

"We both saw how many there were," Em said. "If they're all in bodies... I'm not sure that we can hope to fight them all. We'll lose, Kaia."

"No," Kaia said, shaking her head. She wasn't going to accept that, wasn't going to accept the possibility that the inspector might be lost to them. "No, we'll win. We have to."

"A fight does not respect which side is right," Aunt Keris said. "Only which side has more power, and here, now, it is not us. You know what happened in the fountain square, Kaia. A dozen shadowseers killed, like it was nothing. The four of us will not be able to outfight the shadows. Certainly not in the dark."

"So we're just going to abandon the inspector?" Kaia asked, not quite able to believe that her aunt could be that cruel. Yet she'd done almost the same thing before in Rome, when the inspector had been captured by bounty hunters. She'd been prepared to leave him with them because she'd been utterly focused on the relic.

"If we had a chance of saving him, things would be different," her aunt replied. "But you and Em have already shown that you cannot drive out the shadow that has lodged itself in him."

"We just didn't do it right," Kaia said. "We'll find a way. We'll..."

She was crying, and she hated that she was crying, because that made it look like she was just reacting emotionally, reacting in a way that wouldn't convince her aunt or the others at all.

Olivia put her arms around Kaia.

"I know," Olivia said. "I know you want to help him. But he wouldn't want you to put yourself in that much danger to save him. He wouldn't want you to die, Kaia."

Even Olivia wasn't prepared to go after her father? Was Kaia really the only one willing to do this?

"I'll do this alone if I have to," Kaia said, pulling away from Olivia.

"No," Aunt Keris said, standing and moving to stand between Kaia and the door. "You won't. I will not permit you to throw your life away, Kaia, nor to place the whole world in danger. As both a shadowseer, and as your aunt, I will stop you. I'll lock you in your room before I let anything happen to you."

In that moment, Kaia felt… defeated. Utterly dejected. She thought they'd all come to Athens to put a stop to the shadows, to end this, and now here her aunt was, stopping her from even trying to save the inspector. What was the point of having so much power if she couldn't use it to do some kind of good?

"You could be wrong about the shadows' plans," Kaia said. "What if they *can* open the portal the way they want? What if the full moon rises, and we're left fighting a whole army of shadows?"

Aunt Keris shook her head. "I'm not wrong, Kaia. They can't finish the ritual without the relic, so we keep it from them for tonight, the night when they need it. We sit here and we defend it."

"Defend it?" Kaia said.

Aunt Keris's expression hardened. "Did you think that this would be an easy night of sitting here, Kaia? I have no doubt that once the shadows realize we are not coming to them, they will try to come to kill us and take the relic by force. We will need to protect this place, and be ready to run if we must. At least here, though, we stand a chance."

Kaia hadn't considered the possibility that they might all be in danger there, but it seemed that her aunt had worked it all out.

"So what are we supposed to do?" she asked.

"First, go to your rooms and pack up your things in case we have to leave quickly. Then come down to the safehouse armory and find whatever weapons you can. I will have Casper start to prepare defenses here. We must be prepared to take on any shadows who attack us."

"Will my father be among them?" Olivia asked, sounding worried.

Aunt Keris's tone became more sympathetic.

"My guess is that he will be right at the heart of the attack. They will rely on our reluctance to hurt him as a way to get them close enough to kill us. If any of us hesitates tonight, even for a moment, we are all lost."

Meaning that she wanted them to be ready to kill the inspector? No, Kaia couldn't do it. She *wouldn't* do it. Her aunt had come up with this plan, and to her it probably seemed like a sensible way to save the world, but to Kaia, almost everything about it seemed wrong.

"Go now," Aunt Keris said. "We may not have as much time as I would wish. Remember, we only have to make it to dawn, and their window of opportunity to open the portal will close, at least for now."

Kaia knew that continuing to argue was pointless, so she went upstairs with her sister to the room that they were staying in. She packed away her things, wondering if they would actually have a chance to run once all of this began, and where they would be able to run *to*. As for the whole business of just surviving until dawn... well, what then? They would still have to find a way to deal with the shadows, still have to try to find a way to save the inspector.

Except that her aunt had made it clear that she didn't think that was a priority anymore.

Kaia couldn't let it go so easily. If their plan didn't save the inspector, then what was the point of it? When it came to a choice between saving the world and saving him... well, the world had never shown her any kindness as an orphan, while the inspector had been just about the only person to do so.

Kaia knew in that moment that she couldn't just go along with her aunt's plan. She couldn't sit and wait for the shadows to attack, knowing that the inspector might be killed in that attack. She couldn't just wait while he was out there somewhere, under the control of a shadow.

"We should get ready quickly," Em said. She sounded frightened, as if she were starting to realize just how dangerous everything could be tonight. "I hope Casper is okay."

"Why don't you go down and check?" Kaia suggested.

"What, when he's spending all his time with Cassiopeia?" Em replied.

Kaia shrugged. "He's doing that because he has to guard her. I'm sure he'd much rather spend the time with you."

"Maybe," Em said, but she didn't sound as though she believed it. She certainly didn't make a move toward the door.

"Em, if things are as dangerous as Aunt Keris says, then you should go to him." Kaia felt bad about doing this to her sister, but at the same time, Em probably *should* speak to Casper. "I've seen the way you look at him, Em. It's obvious that you feel something about him, and you've been holding back, but if you don't tell him that now... well, there might not be another chance."

"I..." Em hesitated, and then nodded. "You're right. And it's not like I can just wait for some stupid boy to come and say it all first. I'll be waiting until the shadows have come and gone for that."

She hugged Kaia.

"Thanks, Kaia. And... I just want to say that in spite of the part where there's a chance we'll both be killed by shadows tonight, I'm really glad we found one another."

"I'm glad too," Kaia said. "And... I'm sorry I'm the one who ended up with more of the power, Em."

Em shrugged. "That's just the way things are. And it means that you'll have to destroy more of the shadows when they come. Don't forget to get a weapon from the armory. You'll need it."

She headed downstairs, leaving Kaia alone.

Carefully, Kaia took out the relic, setting it on Em's pillow. Her sister might be able to use it in the coming battle, and her aunt was right, they *couldn't* go up to the Acropolis with it. That would be as good as giving it to the shadows.

But Kaia couldn't just abandon the inspector either. She couldn't just stand there and wait when she could be going up there to try to save him, to try to make a difference. She had to hope that with enough power, enough of an effort, she might be able to push the shadow out of the inspector. Maybe she could even stop all of this before the shadows came to the safehouse.

At the very least, she had to try.

Moving on silent feet, Kaia slipped out of the house into the growing darkness and headed for the Acropolis that sat above the city.

CHAPTER TWENTY

Kaia walked alone through Athens by night, hoping all the time that she was doing the right thing. This was exactly what her aunt hadn't wanted her to do, something none of the others agreed with, and yet Kaia knew that she had to do it. She had to try to save the inspector, whatever it took.

Kaia made her way along the streets of the city, trying not to attract attention as she went. It was quieter here at night than it had been in London, Paris, or even Rome. There were a few tavernas open, and a certain amount of raucous music filtering through into the night air, and a few people making their way along the streets, but mostly, Athens had the feeling of somewhere near abandoned by night.

Whenever Kaia did see someone on the street, she ducked out of sight into a doorway, waiting until they passed. It wasn't just because of all the potential dangers of a strange city at night, but also because Kaia couldn't be sure who might be working for the shadows, or for that bounty hunter she had sent flying. There might even be her aunt, Em, and Olivia out there by now, searching for her.

Kaia couldn't afford any interference right then, couldn't allow anything to slow her down as she went to try to get to the inspector.

She kept her senses extended, trying to pick out any hint of the shadows as she went. Previously, Kaia had been able to feel shadows all around the city, making her worry about where she might find them. Now though, she could only feel their presence up ahead, in the Acropolis. They were gathering there for their ritual, and Kaia found herself wondering exactly what she was walking into.

She had to keep going, though, no matter how many shadows were up there. Knowing that they were there meant that Kaia could move a little quicker through the streets, but she still had to watch out for the possibility of people who had just been paid by the shadows, and for other dangers.

Because she was watching, Kaia was able to catch a glimpse of someone following her. She realized with a start that it was the man who had been hunting for the inspector: Mr. Illingworth. Kaia recognized his squat features and that umbrella that he always carried, and the sight of him made fear rise in her. He'd already made it clear that he was prepared to use violence against her, and that he saw her as a way of getting to the inspector. Then there was the fact that she'd used her powers on him. If he was back again, if that hadn't been enough to scare him off, then there was a good chance of him wanting revenge.

Kaia quickened her step at the sight of him, then ducked into a side alley. There was a perfect spot off to one side where Kaia could hide, and...

...and Mr. Illingworth had already found her and the others hiding once. He'd done it easily because he'd out-thought them. He'd worked out what they were going to do.

So Kaia had to assume that he would work out what she was going to do, too. He would know that she would want to hide. If he really was as clever as the inspector, then Kaia had to assume that he would guess what she was going to do next too, wanting to just keep running.

If the inspector were hunting her, what would Kaia do?

She would do something else. She would go somewhere that he couldn't follow easily. Her advantages were her powers and her smaller size, so Kaia looked around until she found an iron drainpipe, starting to shimmy up it. She suspected that Em would have done it without a second thought, but Kaia had to force herself to do it, trying not to think about what would happen if she lost her grip, or if the drainpipe couldn't hold her weight. Her arms burned with the effort of climbing, but she pulled herself over the edge of the roof.

Kaia was just in time. She saw Mr. Illingworth walk into the alley and immediately go to the spot that Kaia had first thought of as her hiding place. He paused, obviously surprised that she wasn't there, and then kept going down the alley. He clearly thought that Kaia's second choice would be to keep running.

Kaia waited until he was clear, slid down the drainpipe, and headed in the direction of the Acropolis again. The hillside leading to it was steep, with the houses of the city slowly giving way to ancient remains, with broken columns and the structures of ancient homes and temples there as part of the great citadel that it had been. It was like stepping from a modern city into something straight out of the past, the skeletons of old buildings there in silent testament to the long dead. Trees stood between the buildings, a rocky escarpment leading up to the walls of the ancient citadel above.

Kaia could feel the presence of the shadows now, ahead and above her. She guessed that most of them were waiting in the Acropolis, but she could feel other presences closer to her.

She saw the shape of a man hidden back in some of the ruins and felt the shadow there within him. He was obviously there as a guard, there to keep out anyone who might interfere with the shadows' ritual. Perhaps he was even there specifically to wait for Kaia.

She might well be able to take on a single shadow, given her powers. This one didn't feel anywhere near as strong as the one in the inspector. Yet how much sound would that generate in this tomblike, silent place? How much light would flare as Kaia used her powers? It would be like sending up a beacon that told the other shadows exactly where she was.

Kaia couldn't take them all on at once. At least, she didn't think she could, and she certainly didn't want to try if she didn't have to. It was far better to keep moving, and to try to find the inspector without being spotted.

Keeping her head down, Kaia started to move through the trees around the base of the slope that led up to the Acropolis. She went wide around the waiting shadow, straining her senses so that she would pick up on any others that were watching for intruders.

The fact that they had guards like this worried Kaia. It suggested to her that maybe the shadows were going ahead with their ritual, in spite of her aunt's guess that they didn't have everything they needed. If she proved to be wrong about that, then it would just be Kaia, without even the relic, trying to stop whatever the shadows had planned.

Kaia tried not to focus on that. Instead, she kept her thoughts firmly on trying to find the inspector. If she could get to him, maybe this time she would have enough power to free him, and once she did that, the two of them would be able to work out what to do about the rest of it together. Kaia guessed that with his strength of will, the inspector would have learned as much about the shadows' plans as they had learned about his thoughts in the time they'd possessed him.

Kaia just needed to work out how to get close to the inspector. There was an obvious way into the Acropolis, up a long series of steps, but Kaia knew that the shadows would be watching for that. She had to find another way in.

She looked around the base of the Acropolis until she found a ruined section, with a long section of slope leading toward it. Kaia thought she might be able to climb it, although it was going to be far from easy.

At least it would be better than trying to fight her way through all the shadows. Taking them all on would definitely use up too much of

Kaia's power, leaving none left to try to free the inspector from the grip of the shadow.

Gritting her teeth, Kaia started to climb.

The slope was unstable under her feet, so that it felt as if every step slid back half the distance Kaia had made with it. She had to put her hands down on the scree to keep from tumbling down to the bottom, pushing with her legs and pulling with her arms to try to make any kind of progress.

Kaia had to keep going, even as her lungs burned with the effort, and her muscles complained with it. She forced herself to take the next step up the slope, then the next. The walls of the Acropolis were growing closer at least. Just another minute or two of effort, and she would be there. The ruined section of the wall was nearly within reach.

Kaia made it to that section, pulling herself up. She truly had to climb now, using the broken sections of wall for handholds until she could clamber into a gap. Just as she did so, she felt her foot slipping, her foothold giving way.

In that moment, Kaia knew that she was falling, and that fall would hurt, maybe even kill her. The terror of that filled her, along with a deep sense of regret, because she had come there to free the inspector, and now she never would.

A hand closed around her wrist, nearly impossible strength pulling her up. Kaia felt a huge surge of relief as she managed to get her feet on solid ground. That relief quickly gave way to fear as she felt the presence of a shadow.

Not just any shadow. Kaia felt the power of that shadow, felt it and knew that she'd felt that power before. It was immense, almost overwhelming. She scrabbled back, breaking away from the grip on her arm, but she knew even as she did so that it was only because she'd been allowed to do so.

By the light of the full moon, Kaia saw Inspector Pinsley's features staring over at her, a cruel smile playing across his lips.

"Hello, Kaia," he said. "We've been expecting you."

He pulled at her arm, dragging her down a set of steps from the wall into the heart of the Acropolis.

Kaia could see figures all around, lit by the light of the full moon. The figures were young and old, men and women, some dressed in rich clothes, others looking like beggars or soldiers. Kaia could feel the power of the shadows emanating from every one of them.

They'd taken so many people already, those too weak to resist, the powerful who were too corrupt to keep them out, and the simply mad.

There were dozens of them at least, maybe more. Far too many for Kaia to fight all at once.

She could see the markings on the floor of the Acropolis, a large round stone dais with runes set there, glowing with a kind of dark purplish light, flickers of power. Kaia could feel the power in the Acropolis, like a hundred shadowseers or more standing there at once. But there was something else there now, an edge of corruption that Kaia knew was down to the workings of the shadows.

"Did you think I wouldn't know you would come?" the shadow in Pinsley said. "Did you think I didn't arrange all of this specifically so that you would?"

"Arrange?" Kaia said, but then she saw it.

"Letting one shadowseer go from the ambush to get a message out to you? Letting you live when I could have killed you in the shadowseer house? Taking *this* one, knowing that you would follow him? Did you think that any of this was accidental, girl?"

"Why?" Kaia said. "Why lure me here?"

Pinsley gave Kaia a look that made her blood freeze.

"Because your aunt was right: there is a piece missing from our ritual, and that piece is you."

CHAPTER TWENTY ONE

Smiling, Em went back up to the room she shared with Kaia. It had been good to see Casper, and to see the obvious way he reacted to her presence. It was a reminder that he *did* like her, and that maybe…

No, Em couldn't think about that. She and the others had to get through the night first. Em had a heavy club in her right hand, a large knife strapped to her belt, a shotgun set across her back. They were weapons that didn't require a huge amount of training; weapons that she might be able to use successfully, if it came to it.

She hurried back upstairs now. Kaia would need a weapon too, and Em had brought her a spare ironwood stick, heavy and solid enough to drive back an attacker. She used it to knock on the door to their room.

"Are you awake in there?" Em asked, pushing the door open without waiting for an answer. "You were right about Casper. He—"

Em stopped as she saw that the room was empty, with no sign of her sister. Did that mean she was downstairs, getting ready for the possibility of an attack by the shadows? Em didn't know, but she had a sudden bad feeling about all of this.

That feeling only intensified when Em saw the relic sitting there atop her pillow. Kaia had taken it with her everywhere she'd gone so far in their journey through Athens since the moment Aunt Keris had given it to her. She hadn't so much as handed it over to any of the rest of them, let alone left it somewhere like this. Then there was the fact that it was sitting on *Em's* pillow, not on Kaia's. That seemed too much like a gift, or an apology for arguing with her before, or… or a way of saying goodbye.

That thought had Em near to panic, and she snatched up the relic. Instantly, she could feel the power of it, and she stretched out with that power.

Where are you, Kaia? she demanded.

There was no answer.

Kaia, talk to me.

Still, her sister didn't reply. Was she hurt, or worse? No, Em could still feel her there, somewhere on the edge of her consciousness. Kaia just wasn't replying.

Em used the power of the orb to stretch her consciousness out, looking over the city. She might not be as strong as Kaia, but she could still see like this with the help of the relic. She could still make out the darkness of the shadows gathered near the Acropolis, but worse, she could make out the flaring brightness of her sister's power, almost like a miniature sun, making its way up toward the ruins.

She'd gone to the Acropolis. She'd gone to try to save the inspector.

Damn it, Kaia, Em sent. *Don't be so stupid!*

Kaia still didn't provide her with the barest hint of an answer, and Em knew that there was only one thing to do right then.

She ran downstairs, calling out as she went. "Olivia! Aunt Keris! It's Kaia!"

They came running, along with Casper, and even Cassiopeia.

"What is it?" Aunt Keris asked. She was armed now with such a bristling selection of weapons that she seemed ready to take on an army.

"Kaia is heading to the Acropolis," Em said. "She left this behind."

She took out the relic for them to see.

"She wants to go after my father," Olivia guessed. She had a couple of pistols and a long knife strapped to her belt, looking uncomfortable about their presence. "But she doesn't want to risk the relic falling into the hands of the shadows."

"Foolish, *foolish* girl," Aunt Keris said.

"We have to go after her," Em said. "I know you said we couldn't risk going there, and that we couldn't give up our lives for the inspector, but this is different. Kaia isn't controlled by a shadow. We can still help her."

There was a long, drawn out moment of silence, apparently as Aunt Keris made up her mind. In that moment, Em's biggest fear was that her aunt might say no; that she might declare it too dangerous to even attempt to save Kaia, and that she would stop Em from going to try it. In that moment, Em found herself wishing that she'd simply headed out after her sister, because she couldn't save Kaia if her aunt locked her away in her room.

Aunt Keris's grim expression made that seem all the more likely. The only possibility that made sense.

"All right," she said. "Casper, stay here and defend the safehouse. Cassiopeia, stay with him, we can't have you near the shadows. If we do not come back, get messages out to every shadowseer group still out there. Try to prepare them for what's coming."

"We're going to the Acropolis?" Olivia asked.

"I have lost my sister and her husband to the shadows, along with most of my group," Aunt Keris said. "I'll be damned if they are going to take my niece from me too. We're going there, and we're going to get her to safety, if I have to drag her away myself!"

*

Mr. Illingworth was quite annoyed. He was annoyed with himself, and he was annoyed with the girl, Kaia. He had lost her, when as far as he could tell, she was potentially the most valuable individual he might be able to lay his hands on right then.

The manner in which he had lost her was even more annoying. He had been following her, looking for the opportunity to take her, but also working on the assumption that she might lead him to Inspector Pinsley. He still had a job to complete, no matter how much magic was in the world.

He had observed the moment when she had spotted him, of course. That was a simple matter of reading her body language, the changes in her patterns of movement and behavior.

He had continued to follow as she had tried to evade him, moving quickly, and taking a sudden turning designed to give her enough time to hide. At that point, Mr. Illingworth had found himself calculating quickly, working out what the girl would try.

His first hypothesis was that she would hide, and perhaps try to strike out at him as he passed. He established her most likely hiding place almost instantly on entering the alleyway, and approached with his umbrella ready to strike her. He had no wish to kill her, given how valuable she could prove, but he hadn't wanted to give her a chance to lash out at him again with whatever uncanny power she possessed.

Only she hadn't been there. She'd obviously learned from their previous encounter and kept running. Mr. Illingworth had kept going after her, and made it almost the length of another street before he realized that the girl had anticipated that move too. She had out-thought him, and that had rankled in a way that few other things could.

A part of him had wanted to charge through the streets searching for her, yet Mr. Illingworth already knew that was the wrong way to go about things. He needed to think rationally, needed to think about what his subjects wanted to achieve here.

So he considered the situation. Why would a young woman like Kaia be out at night, in the middle of Athens, alone? Presumably not taking the air, not at this hour. Presumably not sneaking out to meet some young man, when they had only been there a brief time. But also probably not doing anything to address whatever broader issue had drawn them all there. She would not be doing that alone.

So why, then?

Mr. Illingworth came to a conclusion quickly: it had to have something to do with the inspector. Something that the others did not believe to be a good idea. Potentially something dangerous.

Of course, that only drove home just how important it had been not to lose her the way he had. Ye he also saw ways back into this. If he could find Pinsley, then the odds were that he would find Kaia too.

He had an idea of where she might head. The rumors about the Acropolis were clear. Yet he didn't head there. A rumor wasn't a sufficient basis for action, not compared to what was possible with a more complete understanding of human nature.

Kaia had crept out alone. Sooner or later, the others would notice, and they would try to find her. Mr. Illingworth guessed that they would have a very good idea of where she had gone, so all he had to do was follow them. More carefully this time, so that they had no idea that he was there.

So he waited in a spot that he had determined was likely outside the place where they were staying, based on the rumors about strangers in the city, and the little information he had been able to glean from informants in the city. Mr. Illingworth assumed that it was only a matter of time before they established that young Kaia was missing, and tried to find her. He also assumed that they would have a clear idea of where she had gone.

It took some time for them to emerge. Apparently, they hadn't noticed her absence quickly, or had spent time trying to work out what to do once they did. Mr. Illingworth spotted the other twin, Emmeline, among the group. If she had half the talents that her sister possessed, she would also be a valuable prize in all of this.

He stalked along behind them, keeping his distance as they made their way through the streets. Simply from the directness with which the three of them moved, he guessed that they had a good idea about where young Kaia had gone. That was good, because Mr. Illingworth didn't want to waste any more time.

Mr. Illingworth kept to the shadows, moving quickly and silently as they all hurried through the city. They were heading uphill, and now he could see the Acropolis ahead, its silhouette stark against the moonlight. It seemed that the rumors were right, and that was where tonight's endeavors would take place.

Mr. Illingworth had no interest in wading into the middle of whatever those activities were. If the business involved the kind of powers that young Kaia had demonstrated, then he was better off on the sidelines. He knew his limitations, and had no intention of endangering his life by being in the wrong place at the wrong time.

No, this was all about finding the *perfect* place. A good hunter did not chase. A good hunter waited. The question now was where. Where would be the right spot in which to wait for Inspector Pinsley to come to him? Once he had Pinsley, he suspected that Kaia would come to him.

Mr. Illingworth bent his mind to the task, making deductions based on the variables that he was aware of. He stared up at the citadel of the Acropolis, considering its contours, and everything that might plausibly happen there.

Once he was sure that he had deduced the correct spot in which to stand, he ambled over, leaned on his umbrella, and waited for his quarry to arrive.

CHAPTER TWENTY TWO

Kaia reeled from the news the shadow possessing the inspector had just given her: that she was the missing part of the ritual all along. Like her aunt, she'd assumed that it would be the relic. She'd thought that by leaving that behind when she came here, she was preventing the shadows from ever achieving their aim, but now it seemed that she had played right into their hands.

"You can't make me help you," Kaia said.

The inspector raised an eyebrow. "Can't we?"

A couple of possessed people started toward Kaia, and she reacted on instinct, summoning her power and throwing it at the one nearest to her, a young man with a mop of dark hair. Her power flooded into him, and the shadow came pouring out through his mouth, only for Kaia's power to wrap around it, ripping it to shreds in a burst of light that made the other shadows flinch back.

"Do you think the loss of one of our kind means that much to us?" the one in Pinsley asked. "Do you think it means that you can stop us?"

More of them advanced on Kaia, and this time her power burst out in a wave, throwing them back, sending them sprawling. They just got up again, though, coming at her once more, as unstoppably as a rising tide. Kaia backed away, her hands raised to protect herself.

Another opponent came at her, and she flung her power into him, driving out the shadow within him. If she could just do it to enough of them, maybe there would be people there who could help her in this fight. This man, a soldier, looked around, blinking, and seemed to realize what was happening. He swung the sword in his hand at another of the possessed people...

He died for it. Without the strength of the shadows behind him, he couldn't keep up as the shadow sidestepped his attack and then struck out violently with a hammer. Kaia felt sickened by that death. Before, when she'd driven shadows out of people, it had *saved* them. Now, a man lay dead on the floor, in the wake of her using her powers.

More shadows closed in on Kaia, and a couple managed to get a grip on her arms. Kaia flung them back with another burst of energy, sending them tumbling among the columns around the dais.

Inspector Pinsley closed on her then and, without thinking about it, Kaia threw everything she had into trying to exorcise the shadow from his body. Her power plunged into him, with Kaia crying out with the effort as she tried to force the shadow from him. She could see the inspector clenching his fists in pain, his features set in determination as the shadow tried to cling onto control of him.

"You will not have him!" Kaia shouted, flinging yet more power into him. "You *will* not."

She had held back before, out of fear of hurting the inspector. Now, though, she didn't hold back. Her power washed over him, washed through him, light burning into all the dark places within, leaving nowhere for a shadow to hide. Kaia was determined to burn every last scrap from the inspector, knowing that it was both the only way to save him and the best way to stop the shadows' plans. If she could exorcise their leader and destroy it, she doubted that the others would be able to open their grand portal and allow their kind to swarm through, empowered to take over humanity.

Kaia threw everything she had at the shadow, not holding back even when she saw blood start to trickle from the inspector's nose. She knew that he would rather suffer that pain than put up with a shadow controlling him, or with the possibility of the shadows taking over the world. She screamed as she continued to pour energy into the shadow, continued to try to drive it out.

It didn't work.

Kaia couldn't sustain the flow of power. She found herself collapsing to her knees with the effort, the light ceasing to pour from her into the inspector. He stood there with an amused expression, casually wiping the blood away from his face. He nodded to the other shadows, and now they were able to grab Kaia, lifting her and holding her by her arms between them so that she was forced to face the inspector.

"We established before that you don't have the power to drive me out," the shadow in Pinsley said. "But thank you for weakening yourself to the point where you can be captured."

"It doesn't make a difference," Kaia said. "I still won't help you with your ritual. I won't help to bring more shadows into the world."

"Oh, I wasn't expecting you to do it *willingly*," the shadow said. "But once I have control of your body, your opinion on the matter won't count for anything. Why did you think I took over the inspector here?"

The shadow had done it to lure her in, to bring her to this place so that she could be captured. It had forgotten one thing, though.

"You still can't possess me," Kaia said. "I don't care how strong you are. I'm not letting you in."

Shadow roiled out of the inspector's mouth, heading for Kaia. She held firm, steeling herself against it as darkness enveloped her, whispers starting around her.

Let me in. Don't you want to be powerful enough to help people? Don't you want to be more than just an orphan girl running away from everything? Let me in, and we can do so much for the world. Let me in.

"No!" Kaia snapped. She could feel the shadow pushing at her from every direction, but it couldn't find a way into her. Kaia wasn't mad, or drugged, or so corrupted that her defenses had broken down. The shadow couldn't touch her, and even as it tried, Kaia let out a flare of power that pushed it back.

It retreated to the inspector's body, controlling him every bit as firmly as before. As it did so, the possessed people who held Kaia wrenched at her arms, making her cry out in pain, her shoulders feeling as if they were about to be wrenched out of their sockets.

"Give in and the pain can stop," the shadow in the inspector said. "Just let me in, and you will never have to feel pain again. I know how much the world has hurt you, Kaia. The inspector's memories tell me all about it. Join with me, and you will know nothing but bliss, forever."

"No!" Kaia snarled back through the pain, determined not to yield even for a second.

The shadow used the inspector's finger to trace down the line of her jaw. "That is easy enough to say now, Kaia, before any real pain has begun, but if you continue to defy us, we will take you and put you in a room where every horrific thing you can begin to imagine will be done to you, and it will be worse, because it will be *this* body doing it to you. We will break you, Kaia."

Kaia tried to contain the terror she felt at those words, tried not to think about the bloodstains or the tools she'd seen in that room in Cassiopeia's house.

"Eventually even the strongest will breaks," the shadow said. "Enough drugs, enough torture, enough humiliation, and there will be nothing left of you to fight back against me. I will drive you mad with it, and I will flow into the cracks that madness leaves."

119

It whispered the threat like a promise from a friend, letting the full horror of the words creep over Kaia slowly. She forced herself to stare over at the inspector in defiance.

"So why don't you?" she demanded. "Why don't you do it? Or are you scared of missing your chance to complete your ritual?"

"You think we can't wait until the next full moon?" the shadow countered. "Just think of the things we could do to you in a whole month, or two, or ten, Kaia. We have waited an eternity for this. A little more time makes no difference."

"Except that shadowseers will start to pour into the city from around the world," Kaia said. "We were the first here, but there will be others. They will fight you. They will rescue me."

The shadow didn't seem impressed. "We can kill shadowseers."

"So it's something else," Kaia said. She hated the thought of the things the shadow was threatening, but she also felt confident. There was some kind of reason why the shadow wasn't simply carrying out its threat, why it hadn't snatched her before and done exactly that kind of thing to Kaia until she broke and let the shadow in.

In that moment, she thought she understood.

"You can't risk it, can you?" Kaia said. "You can't risk the damage that might do to me. You might kill me while you're trying to hurt me enough to let you in, or you might damage something in me that lets me access my powers. You might make me useless to you at the same time as you try to control me. You *can't* force me to do this."

"Can't I?" the shadow snapped, and it drew the inspector's revolver, setting the barrel against Kaia's skull.

Kaia had to force herself to keep staring at the inspector, not to shy away in fear. She was still afraid, still terrified of the prospect that the shadow might pull the trigger, but she forced herself not to show any of that fear.

"If you kill me, you don't get any of what you want. Pull the trigger. You'll *never* get your portal."

The inspector pulled back. "You're right. I can't get you to do what I want by threatening you. Thankfully, your safety isn't the only thing you care about here."

He took a step away from Kaia, and then lifted the pistol to the side of his own head.

"No!" Kaia called out.

"Yes," the shadow snarled. "You will accept me. You will allow me to take over your body, or I will put a bullet through the brain of this one."

"No, you wouldn't!" Kaia said.

"Of course I would," the shadow said. "I have already killed many of your kind. I will survive it, of course, but your precious inspector will die. And afterwards, I *will* have you taken from here to break you slowly, whatever the risks."

Kaia felt more fear for the inspector than she had for herself. She had no doubt now that the shadow would do it, that it would kill the inspector just to get what it wanted.

Kaia understood that logically, she shouldn't do it. Logically, helping the shadows would hurt many, many people. It would potentially transform the world as she knew it, and the whole world had to be worth more than one life. Didn't it?

Yet Kaia couldn't convince herself of that, not when it came to the inspector. He meant too much to her. He'd been the closest person to her for so long now. She'd come here specifically to save him. She couldn't lose him now. She couldn't.

Kaia could see sudden strain on the inspector's face, his hand shaking as if there were conflict taking place within him. Kaia knew just how indomitable the inspector's will was. The shadows wouldn't have been able to get into him without some kind of trickery. Maybe that gave him a greater capacity than most to fight back now.

"Don't do it, Kaia!" he said, the words coming out in a rush. "You can't give them what they want, no matter the—"

Kaia saw his expression change as the shadow reasserted its control.

"Your inspector is a strong man, but he is also foolish. He thinks that you will let him die. He thinks that you will stand there and watch as I put a bullet through his skull. Will you do that, Kaia?"

"No," Kaia said. In spite of the inspector's words, she knew she couldn't do it. She couldn't let him die. And maybe, just maybe, if he could fight back, so could she. "No. Let him go. Let him live, and you can have me."

"Good," the shadow said, and flowed out of the inspector toward her.

This time, Kaia didn't resist.

CHAPTER TWENTY THREE

Pinsley felt the moment when the shadow started to leave his body and cried out, trying to beg Kaia not to do this. His mouth wouldn't do what he wanted, though, wouldn't let him tell her not to, tell her the trick that the shadow was trying to play on her.

He'd felt the moment when the shadow had relaxed its grip on him. He'd thought that he was fighting back against it, but as it had reasserted its control, Pinsley had known that the shadow had allowed it. It had given Kaia that hope that it might be able to fight it. It had given her another reason to accept its ultimatum, and that reason had been a lie.

The shadow poured out of him and straight into Kaia. It flowed into her, filling her, *becoming* her. It took her form, and Pinsley saw her power flaring around her, saw the moment when she tried to use a burst of her powers to destroy it even as it tried to take her over.

Then that glow of power faded, and shadows deepened around Kaia's eyes, lending her a sinister look.

Pinsley realized that he still had his pistol pressed to his own skull. He took it from there and pointed it at Kaia, hating it even as he did it.

"What are you doing, Inspector?" the shadow asked. "You aren't going to hurt me, are you? It's Kaia."

"No," Pinsley said. "It isn't, not anymore."

"Ah, I see," the shadow said. "You think you're going to save the world. You think that you have it in you to shoot a young woman between the eyes. A young woman you care about. A young woman you see as a daughter, as much as your *real* daughter."

"I will do it if I have to," Pinsley said. He'd seen the alternative in the thoughts of the shadow. It amounted to the end of the world, the end of humanity as they knew it. The shadows could only achieve that, though, if they had Kaia. "I know what you intend."

"And I know *you*," the shadow replied. "I saw all that you are, while I was a part of you. The man so traumatized by his time in the Crimean Peninsula that he resigned his commission in the army rather than have to kill again. The man who gave up his entire career rather than abandon Kaia to travel alone, even though you did not believe her then. A man who will not pull that trigger to save the world, because that will mean ending Kaia's life."

Pinsley hesitated, finger on the trigger, trying to force himself to do this by sheer effort of will. He was a man of reason, a man of logic, and logic dictated that the only way to save humanity now was to fire. One life, even Kaia's, couldn't be set against the lives of millions.

He told himself all of that, and he still couldn't bring himself to do it. The shadow was right: he loved Kaia the way he loved his own daughter. He couldn't kill her, not for this, not for *anything*. She might have accepted a monster into herself, but it was still Kaia he would be killing.

Pinsley's hands tensed on the revolver in one last effort to do what was necessary, then he flung it from himself, sending it clattering somewhere among the ruins.

The shadows came for him then, and his next thought was to simply grab Kaia and carry her away from there. The shadow in her would make her stronger and more dangerous, of course, but she was still small enough and light enough that he could hoist her over his shoulder if he had to. At that point, he would have to outrun the shadows, but to save her, he would try it.

He lunged at Kaia to try to tackle her, only for her to fling up a hand and her power to come rippling out. It flung Pinsley back almost casually, sending him flying through the air. He rolled when he hit the ground, missing a column by inches, and came up barely in time to block a punch as one of the possessed people came at him.

Pinsley did his best to fight back, lashing out with fists and elbows, but the problem was that there were simply too many foes to take on at once. They grabbed for him, lifting him bodily and dragging him back toward Kaia.

The shadow looked at him coldly through her eyes. "We don't need him anymore. Get rid of him."

Pinsley struggled as the possessed people carried him away from Kaia to the edge of the Acropolis's walls, a slope below leading down to the city.

"Wait!" Pinsley called out. "Kaia, if you're in there—"

They threw him from the wall before he had a chance to finish.

Pinsley hung in the air for an eternity before he hit the slope. He started to slide down it, the ground loose beneath him, and he realized that he was sliding toward a bigger drop-off, one that would see him fall down fifty feet or more to the city below. It was certainly more than enough to kill him.

Away to his right, Pinsley spotted a flat section of what looked like firm ground. He scrambled desperately toward it, unable to arrest his downward momentum, but at least trying to move sideways as he slid. If he missed that flat section, he was going to plummet to his death…

His hands closed on it, and Pinsley pulled himself up, rolling to a stop. Every part of his body hurt right then, battered and bruised by the fall, yet as far as he could tell, Pinsley hadn't actually broken anything. He sat up painfully.

As he did so, he saw a man making his way onto the flat section of rock from the other side, obviously having clambered up from below. There was something squashed, almost toad-like, about his features, and he wore a linen suit and carried an umbrella. He jabbed the sharp point of the latter into the dirt of the escarpment, leaving it standing there the way a race-goer might have left a shooting stick to sit on.

"Inspector Pinsley, I presume?" he said in English.

The simple fact that he spoke English caught Pinsley a little by surprise, after days of dealing with Greek from everyone else in the city. Pinsley didn't think this man was one of the shadows, there to finish him off, if only because they all seemed to be back above. That still left the worrying question of just who this man was, though.

"It seems you have the advantage of me, sir," Pinsley said. He dusted his jacket off carefully.

"Yes, it rather appears that I do," the other man replied. Pinsley saw his hand dip into a pocket and come out with a snub-nosed revolver, a Webley, if Pinsley was any judge of such things.

"Who are you, and what do you want?" Pinsley asked, leaving aside politeness.

"Can you not deduce it, sir?" the man asked, like some Oxford don in a tutorial, waiting to be impressed by a student. "I have heard great things about your deductive powers, almost equal to my own. I should like to see them for myself."

Pinsley wasn't in a mood to indulge this man's games, not when Kaia was in the grip of a shadow above. Yet, with a gun pointed at him, Pinsley wasn't sure that he had any other choice.

"Your accent says that you are English," he reasoned aloud. "You know my name, which suggests you may have come looking for me specifically. Given that I have already run into a pair of bounty hunters on my travels, it seems reasonable that you might be another."

"Ah, but *who*?" the man said, obviously still waiting to be impressed.

"The first two failed," Pinsley said. "Yet you are here alone. That suggests that you are either very foolish or very confident in your abilities. I assume that it is not the former. You have spoken about your powers of deduction…"

A name came into Pinsley's mind, the name of a man famed for his intelligence, his relentlessness, and occasionally his cruelty. The name of a man who made much of his living hunting down others.

"Am I addressing Mr. Frederick Illingworth?" he guessed.

The toad-faced man smiled. "Ah, perhaps you *are* clever enough to be interesting. Tell me, sir, what brings you to the Acropolis?"

He chatted as calmly as if they were taking afternoon tea at his club.

"You wouldn't believe me if I told you," Pinsley said.

"I might," Mr. Illingworth replied. "Given that I have already had a taste of the… abilities your young ward Kaia possesses. Your Superintendent Hutton believes your travels to be random and chaotic. Having seen something of the more uncanny side of things, I have come to believe that they are anything but."

"Very well," Pinsley said. "I am at the Acropolis because a group of incorporeal beings have possessed many people, and are seeking to open a portal here through which to summon more of their number, using Kaia to do it. I say to you, sir, if we allow this, then the whole of the mortal world will fall to them."

"Hmm," Mr. Illingworth said. He didn't exhibit the shock that most people would have, having been told such a thing. "A most difficult situation."

"And one that you must allow me to get back to," Pinsley said.

"Must?" Mr. Illingworth shook his head at that. "Oh, no. I really think not. No, I took a job to bring you in, you see, and I mean to do so. Please place your hands behind your back so that I might cuff you, Inspector."

"Did you not hear a word I just said?" Pinsley demanded. "Forces above us mean to end the entire human world!"

"And I will deal with that shortly," Mr. Illingworth said. "You have hinted that they require your ward to finish things. Well, once I have secured you, I will go up there and put a bullet in her head. That should resolve things nicely. A pity, when I rather hoped to capture her to study, but there will be other opportunities. That sister of hers, for a start."

He said it as if killing Kaia were nothing, as if *she* were nothing.

"I will not allow that," Pinsley said, standing in the other man's way.

"Now, see sense, Inspector," Mr. Illingworth said. "Do not think for a moment that I will hesitate to kill you. I am not burdened by a police inspector's conscience."

Nor by any hint of human decency, as far as Pinsley could see. This was a man who traded only in reason.

"If you fire that gun, every shadow above us will hear it," Pinsley said. "There is no way that you will escape, let alone succeed in getting close enough to harm Kaia. If I have to take a bullet from you to protect her, do you think *I* will hesitate?"

He saw Mr. Illingworth consider him carefully. "No, I rather doubt that you will. Still, there are other options."

Pinsley saw the odious man put the revolver away in his pocket, taking off his linen jacket and hat and setting them atop his umbrella as if it were a hat stand in a hall. As he did it, Pinsley slipped off his own long coat, not wanting to be encumbered by it for what was to come.

Then he saw Mr. Illingworth slip something that shone over his hand. A set of brass knuckles, glinting in the moonlight.

"Oh, did you think I would fight *fair*, sir?" Mr. Illingworth said with a laugh as he started to circle Pinsley, hands up.

"Not for a moment," Pinsley said, and rushed him.

Illingworth dodged that initial rush, moving with surprising speed for a man of his bulk. He slammed a punch into Pinsley's ribs, hard enough to send agony flowing through the inspector, but Pinsley kept going.

He snapped a jab into Illingworth's face, following it up with a cross that the other man slipped aside from, trying to send a blow of his own crashing into Pinsley's skull. The inspector barely ducked it, then got his hands in the way in time to parry a knee aimed at him.

He pushed Illingworth away, snapped out another jab, and this time dove in for a tackle, wanting to test the man's wrestling. Illingworth got his weight back, though, striking Pinsley a blow alongside the ear with the hand that didn't have the brass knuckles. Pinsley's head swam, but he kicked out at Illingworth, buying himself some space in which to clear it.

"I can read your every move, Inspector," Mr. Illingworth said. "There is no *point* to trying to fight me."

Pinsley thought of Kaia, and what this man had threatened to do to her. "There is *every* point."

He charged in again, firing in blows, not caring about those that came in return. He clinched with Illingworth, then slammed a series of uppercuts into his body and head, feeling his knuckles connect with bruising force. He took one blow from the brass knuckles, blocked a second, and then got in a head butt that the sergeant who had taught him to fight back in the Crimea would have been proud of. Illingworth went staggering back, casting aside the brass knuckles as if they were worthless.

"Enough of this," he snarled, snatching up that umbrella of his and holding it as if he were a fencer holding a foil in the salle. The tip of it certainly looked sharp enough.

Pinsley barely dodged the first blow, rolling and picking up his coat as he went. He held it out in front of him like a matador's cape, trying to tangle and distract with it. Still, Illingworth jabbed at him with the umbrella, forcing Pinsley back, pinning him against the edge of the drop to the city. There was nowhere to go, nowhere to move that he could avoid what would undoubtedly be a last fatal thrust.

Pinsley flung his coat, hoping that it would distract Illingworth, but the other man only batted it aside with his free hand, over the edge of the drop. Illingworth lunged, and Pinsley found himself thinking about Keris in that moment, thinking about all the things he might have said to that fascinating woman if only he'd had more time.

Then he found himself thinking about the way she fought, never quite there to hit, twisting away like a ghost. He had one chance, one slim, barely there opportunity to survive this.

Pinsley wasn't as agile as Keris, but at least he could throw himself flat as Illingworth lunged, slamming into the dirt, ignoring the agony in his ribs as he did it. He knew that if Illingworth read this movement, he would simply stop and stab down at Pinsley, but it was the only chance he had.

Pinsley gazed up at Illingworth and saw the moment when the other man realized, too late, what Pinsley was doing. He tried to stop his lunge, but the momentum of it was already too great, and the movement carried him forward, his foot catching against Pinsley's prone form so that he tripped.

That trip sent him stumbling forward, into the one place where he had no space to stumble. Pinsley saw the other man's arms pinwheel for a moment, and then Mr. Illingworth was tumbling out into space, falling down into the city below.

Pinsley lay there for a moment or two, breathing hard. He wanted nothing more than to lie there forever right then, but he knew he couldn't. Mr. Illingworth had put his Webley back in his coat, and with that weapon, Pinsley might actually have a chance of getting to Kaia again to save her.

Struggling to his feet, he grabbed it and set it around his shoulders, feeling the weight of other things in the garment's pockets. There would be time enough for those later.

For now, he had to get to Kaia.

CHAPTER TWENTY FOUR

Em didn't so much lead the way to the Acropolis as hurry out in front of the others, so determined to get to her sister that Aunt Keris and Olivia had to run to keep up. She'd been determined to keep away from the place since the start of all this, determined to avoid even the remotest possibility that she and Kaia might be dragged into performing the shadowseers' ritual, but now Em ran toward the place as fast as she could.

As she approached the lower slopes of the hill leading up to it, though, Aunt Keris put a hand on her shoulder.

"Quietly now. We can't help Kaia if we get caught. You can feel that there are shadows ahead?"

Em could. Two shadows were nearby, and as she strained her eyes, she saw a couple of possessed people waiting by the foot of the steps leading up to the Acropolis, obviously there to guard against intruders.

Em's first instinct was to charge them, but she knew that would only alert the others above. Instead, she crept around to the side with her aunt and Olivia, moving past the shadows and slipping onto the stairs beyond them.

She made her way upwards. Under other circumstances, the Acropolis would have been a spectacular sight, a large complex of ruins that probably wouldn't still have been standing if it had been in the relentlessly modernizing environments of London or Paris. Em could see large stone buildings supported by marble columns, a whole fortress's worth of walls and defenses.

Her only focus right then was on how she could slip through them to get to her sister. Kaia was up there somewhere, Em could feel her power, but she could also feel the presence of far too many shadows gathered around her.

Em took out the long ironwood club she'd selected as a weapon. She would fight her way through as many of the shadows as she had to in order to get to Kaia. Em felt bad about the possibility of hurting ordinary people who simply had the misfortune to be possessed, but when it came to saving her sister, Em wasn't going to hesitate. She was sure that the possessed people wouldn't hold back from hurting or killing her, even for an instant.

Em and the others made their way into the Acropolis, moving quietly, trying to keep out of sight. There were so many shadows around now that it was hard to chart a path between them, Em's powers letting her pick out their locations easily enough, but then having to find a route through them that wouldn't get any of their small group instantly spotted.

She saw a set of steps leading up onto the walls of the Acropolis and took them, wanting to see if she could spot Kaia. Her sister was here somewhere, toward the center of it all, but Em wanted to actually see her, wanted to work out what it would take to get to her.

She looked down from the walls and saw her sister standing on a broad stone dais, at the center of a collection of columns that must once have held a stone roof. Her arms were raised and her eyes were closed, while possessed people stood all around her in a broad circle. Was she trying to use her powers to fight them off, or exorcise all of them at once? If so, why weren't they attacking her? With so many shadows around her, it was hard to pick apart Kaia's power from the shadows around her, but it was there, light flaring around her in a glow that lit up the courtyard of the Acropolis.

Whatever the reason, Em knew that she had to get to her sister. She had to try to help.

I'm coming, Kaia! Em sent, and then found a spot to scramble down into the courtyard.

Almost instantly, one of the possessed came at her, a large man wielding a butcher's cleaver. Em dodged out of the way, swinging her club hard into his knee so that he went down. She grabbed the relic from her pocket, and her power flared in response, letting her fling back the next of the possessed to come at her. She might not have her sister's raw power, but the relic helped to make up for that, giving Em access to deep wells of energy that she hadn't had before. Em used that energy like a battering ram, flinging back those of the possessed who came at her.

Gunshots sounded around her, and dirt spurted up around Em's feet as bullets barely missed her. She saw several of the possessed firing pistols and old rifles, and had to duck back behind a column to avoid being a target. Em was only just in time, stone chips flying from it as bullets hit it, one after another.

She saw Olivia firing back then, holding a pistol in either hand while advancing with surprising ferocity, given that she was not trained for any of this. Em saw one of the possessed fall, clutching his shoulder, then saw another's gun fly right out of his hand as a bullet hit it. It seemed that the Pinsley family had at least one good shot in it after all.

Still, Em could see the possessed advancing on her. One reached out for Olivia, but then Aunt Keris was there, flipping the woman over her hip, then striking out at another of the possessed with a staff. She kept attacking, and Em stepped out from her cover, sending out another wave of power that threw more of the possessed from their feet.

Em could still see Kaia at the heart of a ring of the possessed, still with her hands raised and her eyes closed. One terrifying thought came to her: was Kaia trying to undertake the shadowseers' ritual to destroy the shadows? No, she couldn't! It would kill her!

Em ran for her sister, knocking aside more of the shadows, determined to get there to save her. She ducked under the sweep of a woodcutting axe, threw herself flat as more shots went over her head, and then flung back a large possessed man who tried to grab her.

She'd reached the circle of the possessed now. They turned to Em, trying to keep her out, but Em used her powers to batter them out of the way. With the relic in her hand, she had the strength to do it now. She broke through their ranks and stood opposite her sister, hoping she was in time to help her.

Only now that Em was past the possessed people, she could feel the horrible truth of it. Shadowy energy whirled amid Kaia's brightness, entwined with it, a *part* of it. Kaia had been possessed by a shadow.

"No!" Em said, grabbing for Kaia as if she might be able to drag her out of there.

Kaia's eyes snapped open and she parried Em's hand away, then struck her with an open palm to the center of the chest, sending her sprawling. Em rolled to her feet in time to see Kaia staring at her with a cruel smile that didn't belong on her features.

"Hello, Em," she said. "Come to save me?"

"Let my sister go!" Em snarled, and lashed out with all the power she could channel through the relic, determined to force the shadow out of Kaia.

Kaia raised a hand and her own power leapt to meet Em's, light meeting light, the two forces burning against one another in a torrent that seemed to hold incalculable force. Em had to brace her feet against the power of it, and she saw Kaia doing the same, the two of them suddenly engaged in a pushing match of powers where the first to give way would probably find herself blasted from her feet.

"You can't win, Em," the shadow said, in Kaia's voice. "You know I'm stronger than you. I always have been. I'm the one who matters.

You're just… the spare. The one there to help out. The one nobody will remember."

Em knew what the shadow was doing, using the knowledge it had gained from Kaia's mind to try to hurt her, to try to weaken her resolve enough that it could win. The very fact that it needed to do so gave Em confidence, because it suggested that the shadow couldn't just overwhelm her in one go.

"Why are you even fighting?" the shadow demanded. "I know what you're like, Em. I know you have darkness inside you, that you like the violence, that you want to act as you wish. You were born to be like us."

"I'll never be one of you," Em replied and redoubled her efforts to push power out into her sister.

Em knew that Kaia was stronger, but Em held the relic now, and that counted for a lot. She pushed that power out, holding the orb out in front of her like a shield, focusing her energy through it to amplify her efforts.

She and Kaia both inched forward, moving toward one another pace by pace. Em could feel the strain of trying to channel that much power, could feel sweat starting to drip from her brow with the effort. She leaned into the power, continuing to push forward, determined to drive that power back into her sister.

They got closer and closer, little by little, until they were only a couple of feet apart, then inches. Finally, Em felt Kaia's hand make contact with the orb…

In that instant, Em realized her mistake. Just as the relic had amplified her power, it amplified Kaia's as well. Where an instant before, Em's power had been balanced with Kaia's, now her sister's power was overwhelming. It flung her back, so that she lost her grip on the orb, sending her sprawling, and now the possessed around Em grabbed her, holding her helplessly between them.

She looked around and saw that they also had Aunt Keris and Olivia. Aunt Keris had bruises on her face, while Olivia was down on her knees with her arms twisted behind her.

"Did you really think you could stop us?" the shadow possessing Kaia asked. "Did you really think you had the strength?" The shadow laughed. "But don't worry, we're not going to kill you. There are far better things to do with you. When the first of our kind come through, you will be blessed. You will be among the first to be taken, by some of the strongest of our kind. You will become more. You will become *perfect*."

Kaia stepped back from Em, raising her arms again, and now she had the relic raised in her hand. Em could feel the power pouring through it now, entwined with the dark energy of the shadows.

That energy flowed down into runes carved around the dais, so that they glowed with a purplish black light, the world around them seeming to twist and distort with the rippling energy from them. Em could feel a pressure building in her head, like a storm was coming.

Em saw the space above the dais start to twist, the world itself starting to tear apart. A hole tore in the sky itself, a darkness far deeper than the night around it showing beyond that gap. The world of the shadows was there, and Em could see a tidal wave of shadows pouring toward it.

There was nothing they could do to stop it now.

CHAPTER TWENTY FIVE

Kaia was trapped. Her own body had become a prison, her mind enclosed by walls of shadow that she couldn't breach, her will powerless to control her body.

The strangest thing was that there was a landscape here in the interior of her mind, a strange, shadowy reflection of a London, everything rendered in shades of gray and deep blues, no light leaching into it from the outside.

The outside world was above her, what must have been the view from her own eyes hanging in the sky, the sounds of it still coming to Kaia from all around. She could feel the movement of the power within her, too, and even that didn't seem to be under her control.

It meant that she'd been forced to watch as she had begun the ritual the shadow had created. She'd been able to feel the way it had twisted her power, changing it, using it in ways it had never been intended to be used. It had wrapped that power up in shadow and turned it into something else, something darker.

The worst part was that the shadow was there with her, even as it controlled her. There was a girl there who looked just like her, every feature identical, only she was made of wisps of shadow, and had a cruel twisted expression.

"They think they can help you," the shadow said. "They think they can free you."

Then she heard something that made her stop.

"Kaia, that's enough!"

Kaia heard the inspector's voice and saw him walking into the Acropolis, dressed incongruously in a linen coat that wasn't his.

"Kaia," the inspector called out, still approaching. "You have to fight. You are stronger than the shadow. You *can* break free of this."

"You would think *he* of all people would understand," the shadow said. "He knows what it is like to be controlled. Perhaps I should have us kill him. Would you like that, Kaia?"

"No!" Kaia shouted, throwing herself at the shadow. It flung her back easily.

"Watch," the shadow said.

Kaia heard the next words coming with her own voice, saw herself gesturing to the shadows out there.

"Take him. Hold him. He can join the others. He can become one of us."

Kaia saw the possessed leap forward at the inspector. He struck out at one of them, fired a revolver at a second, but then they were on him, grabbing him, holding him in place.

"You can fight this, Kaia," the inspector said. "You are not alone anymore. You're not an orphan without anyone. We're here for you."

As he said it, he managed to break free an arm. He took hold of Aunt Keris's hand, the two of them standing there together, seeking comfort in one another.

"Come on, Kaia!" Em called out. "Fight back!"

Kaia tried, but she didn't know how to begin. She tried to exert her will, tried to make her body do what she wanted, but it wouldn't respond, wouldn't do what she wanted.

"They don't understand," the shadow said. "Ignore them. We have a ritual to complete."

Kaia saw her own body moving toward the center of the dais again, felt herself raising her arms, felt the power rising once more. She could see the opening of the portal, but there were still steps to the ritual that the shadow wanted to complete, still things it wanted to do that would make its kind stronger as they came through.

"You have the power to fight this," Aunt Keris said. "Kaia, if you're in there, you do not have the weaknesses that let the shadows take others. You are stronger than anyone I know."

Kaia saw the swirling darkness of the portal, saw the swarm of shadows heading toward the world. She knew that if they reached it, the first thing they would do would be to pour into the inspector and the others, flowing into the people she loved and taking them over. They would become no more than puppets. Kaia couldn't allow that.

"Come on, Kaia!" Olivia called out. "You can do this. Fight!"

Kaia leapt at the shadow, throwing herself at it with all the force she could muster. She struck at it, and it struck back, but Kaia twisted aside from the blow. She hit the shadow form, and it recoiled, looking slightly surprised as Kaia did it.

"You can't hurt me, not here," it said. "This isn't real."

"This is my mind," Kaia said, striking out at the shadow again. "And it is as real as I *say* it is."

She hit the shadow again and again, not relenting, driving it back. The shadow girl in front of her recoiled in pain and shock.

Then she started to hit back. Punches came at Kaia, and kicks, striking out at her hard enough that she recoiled in agony.

"Fight, Kaia!" Em called out, and then Kaia saw her reach out with her powers. That power flooded into Kaia, and Kaia saw the gold of her sister's power flood through the shadow city, providing the only hint of color in this otherwise shadow-filled place.

By that light, Kaia struck out at her shadow self, kicking and hitting with all the skills she'd learned from her aunt. The shadow countered those blows, parrying them or stepping aside, none of the strikes getting through in spite of Kaia's best efforts.

"I know everything you know. I am everything you are," the shadow said. "You cannot win. There is nothing you have that I do not."

It struck back then, knocking Kaia down, so that she was left on her knees, staring up at the shadow, breathing hard. It would have been so easy to give in then. So easy to just stay there, letting the shadow complete its dark version of the ritual, bringing its kind into the world while Kaia could do nothing to stop it.

"I have one thing that you don't," Kaia said. "I have a family that loves me."

Kaia reached out with her power, reached out for her connection to Em. That connection meant that she was never truly alone. That connection meant that she knew, every minute of the day, that she had a sister.

She reached for that connection, and she pulled. The shadow tried to stop her, tried to close down that link, but there were some connections that couldn't be broken, no matter how hard it tried.

Em was there then, standing beside Kaia in the shadow world. She took one look at the shadow and brought her hands up ready to fight.

"Leave my sister alone!"

She and Kaia both leapt at the shadow together, striking out with fists and feet. It might know their moves, but that didn't mean that it could deal with both of them attacking together, striking at it from either side, never giving it enough space in which to recover. Whenever it whirled to face Kaia, Em struck out. Whenever it tried to deal with Em's attacks, that gave Kaia the room she needed to hit it.

Little by little, the two drove it back.

"You can't beat me," it said. "I am within you. A part of you."

"*Here* I can beat you," Kaia said. "We can beat you, together."

She raised her hand, golden light pouring out of it in a jet that slammed into the shadow. Em raised hers at the same time, her power striking the shadow from the other side.

It screamed as the light struck it, lashing out with tendrils of shadow that struck like dark whips through the air. One struck Kaia and she stumbled, but Em was there to help her up, and the two of them blasted the shadow with energy again.

They were fighting their way through the darkened city now, pressing the shadow back and trying to cut off the places that it had to run. It struck out again with those tendrils of energy toward Kaia and she dodged, countering with her own power once again.

They reached a spot in front of a twisted, gothic church, so creepy and dark that it took Kaia a moment to realize that it was a version of St. Michael's church where she had stayed in London with Reverend Faulkner and his sister Lottie. Kaia saw a well set before it, and the shadow stood its ground in front of it, as if trying to keep them away from it. A strange golden glow came from within that well, and Kaia knew what it had to be:

It was a representation of her power.

Draw it off, Kaia sent to her sister.

How am I supposed to do that? Em sent back, but even as she did so, she attacked the shadow, throwing everything she had at it. She struck out at the shadow with her fists and with her power, dodging back as the shadow struck for her, forcing it to follow.

As it moved away from the well, Kaia dove for it, making it to the edge and looking down. She saw the power there, glowing with golden light. Kaia stood on the edge of the well then, really hoping that she knew what she was doing.

She dove in.

For a second or two, it was as if she was drowning in her power. It suffused her utterly, seeming to take up every iota of Kaia's being. But that was what she wanted. She *wanted* it to be all consuming, to fill her. To leave no room for the shadow.

Kaia blinked, and in that moment, she was standing in the middle of the Acropolis, with a portal to the shadows' world above her. Kaia could feel her power pulsing through her until it felt as though she might burst with it.

She opened her mouth and screamed, and with that scream, the shadow that had been controlling her poured out, forced up into the open air like smoke. It seemed to take forever to leave her, a huge cloud of it filling the sky around the portal, blotting out the stars above.

Then Em was running to her, kicking away the shadows who held her.

"Kaia? Kaia, can you hear me? Is it you?"

"I'm me," Kaia said. "I'm me again."

She should have felt nothing but relief in that moment. The only problem was that, looking up, it was impossible to feel that relief. Not when the shadow still hung in the air there. Not when the portal was still open, threatening to disgorge enough shadows to overwhelm humanity.

Kaia could feel the shadows' ritual, standing on the cusp of completion now, the power continuing with its own momentum, so that Kaia wasn't sure that it was possible to stop it.

Or maybe it was. Kaia could think of one way. She just hated the thought of what it might mean. She took out the relic and stared at it, its gold and silver segments whirling together so fast it seemed almost impossible.

"Kaia?" Em said. "Kaia, why are you staring at the relic like that?"

"I think… I think we need to perform the ritual, Em."

CHAPTER TWENTY SIX

Kaia stood beneath the portal, feeling the ebb and flow of the power, the shadows' dark ritual having taken the original design of the shadowseers and twisted it to a much more deadly purpose.

It's too late, the shadow that she had just expelled from her body hissed above her and the others. *You might thrust me out of your mind now, but we will take you again soon enough.*

Kaia knew with absolute certainty that it was true. The ritual was almost complete, the power flowing into the runes already. The shadow had seen into her while it occupied her body, but she had seen into it too, and she knew that it would only be minutes more before a horde of shadows overwhelmed the world, empowered to possess anyone they wished.

Kaia could only think of one way to stop that. She lifted the relic, ready to begin the ritual this place had been designed for, the one the first shadowseers had intended to wipe shadows from the world. The one that had saved humanity even when it hadn't worked fully.

The one that had already killed pair after pair of shadowseer twins.

"Kaia, no!" Em said. "You can't do this! You can't just throw your life away!"

"I have to," Kaia replied. "If I don't do this, humanity will die."

"We'll find another way," Aunt Keris said.

But there *was* no other way. If there were, Kaia would gladly have taken it. She didn't want to die. There was so much she hadn't seen yet, or done.

Yet at the same time, she had already seen more of the world than she had ever expected to as an orphan in London. She had been to cities whose names might as well have been those of mythical lands, given what she knew of them. She had fought monsters and been kissed by a prince, even if he had turned out to be a murderer. She had helped to uncover mysteries, and done things that no one her age should have been able to do.

Kaia didn't want to die, she was afraid, but if that was what it took to save the world, then that was what she would do.

Kaia started to focus her power into the relic, knowing that it was designed for this. It was meant to be used here, in this place. The silver and gold of it spun faster and faster, until they became a shining blur in her hand.

"Kaia!" Inspector Pinsley cried out, emotion cracking his usually implacable façade.

"I have to do this," Kaia said, as she kept pouring her power into the relic.

She felt the moment when that power started to connect to the lines and symbols embedded in the Acropolis, prepared against exactly this moment. She felt the power start to flow through those channels the way water might flow down a series of irrigation ditches, each one filling and glowing with golden light that shone against the dark.

Stop her! Kill her!

Dimly, Kaia was aware of the possessed starting forward, of her aunt, the inspector, and Olivia moving to stand in their way. Kaia heard shots and shouting, but they were distant things. She had to focus on the ritual. Even her fear for the people she loved couldn't distract her right then.

Kaia could feel the way the shadows had changed the ritual. She could see the twists that they had put into the markings, and Kaia's first job was to burn through them, taking them away so that she wasn't just fueling the shadows' dark ritual. It seemed to take an eternity, but Kaia knew it must only have been seconds.

In those seconds, the part of Kaia that wasn't performing the ritual saw her aunt swing a knee into a man's face, saw Olivia fighting hand to hand with a woman, and the detective trying to fend off three people at once.

Burning through the runes felt like burning through a part of herself. It hurt, but Kaia accepted the pain, kept going in spite of it. She had to do this, no matter what it cost her.

She felt the shadows' changes fade, and now the full beauty of the ritual was revealed, in layer upon layer of workings, each one designed to add to a shadowseer's power. Each of them felt similar to the relic Kaia held, and she knew then that it was the key to all of them, the only way to truly understand them.

Kaia kept pouring power out of herself, along the paths that the ancient shadowseers had put in place, and felt the power of the ritual start to grow.

"Hurry, Kaia!" her aunt called out. She was fighting three of the possessed now, struggling to keep them all away from her. The inspector was being dragged down by more of them, in spite of his efforts to fight back.

Kaia couldn't do anything to help them, couldn't take her attention away from the ritual. In that moment, she *was* the ritual, turned into something far more than a single human, far bigger even than the Acropolis. Kaia's powers stretched out, and she saw...

Everything.

The world stretched out around Kaia, and she saw it in terms of waves of energy. She understood the intrinsic power of the world, understood the flow of it, because she was a part of that flow.

She saw the shadows too, not just in Athens, but in every corner of the world. She saw them walking around in human form, lurking formless in dark places, corrupting those who were too weak to stop them.

Kaia saw the portals, too. The one in Athens was the largest, but there were others, so many others. Kaia knew that she had to stop them.

Kaia reached out with her powers, reached out with the relic, and it seemed almost easy to close the first of those portals, somewhere deep in a jungle, far from the prying eyes of men. Her power flicked out, and another slammed closed, in a set of caverns down beneath Edinburgh.

Kaia reached for portal after portal, her power flowing out almost automatically, without her even thinking about it. She realized in that moment that she wasn't so much choosing to use it as simply riding that power, following where it went as it flamed out across the world, burning away the shadows' ways into the world.

It burned her too. Kaia felt a twinge of pain as she closed down the shadows' portals, felt her body suddenly shaking with the strain. Kaia realized then that, even with her immense strength, she didn't have enough to do this alone.

She *wasn't* alone, though. Even as Kaia thought it, she felt the presence of her sister there with her, Em's power adding to Kaia's, entwining with it, becoming more than the sum of the parts.

I thought you didn't want to do the ritual, Kaia sent to her.

I don't, but I'm not going to let you do this alone, Em sent back. *I just hope you know what you're doing.*

Together, their power rippled out, and Kaia felt portals closing, one after another. She felt shadows being pushed back, forced through those portals and cast from the world. The power she and Em shared spread like a golden dawn over the corners the shadows occupied, leaving no space for them.

Still, Kaia could feel the effort of doing so much. She was aware of the sweat dripping from her brow, of a heat rising within her. That heat was great enough that it burned, and that burning *hurt*.

Kaia heard Em cry out in her head. It was all she could do to maintain her grip on the ritual. Not that losing that grip would have stopped it. By now, the ritual seemed to have a momentum of its own, so that Kaia and Em were carried along by it. Yet if Kaia lost control, even for an instant, she knew that it would kill both of them, just as it had so many before them.

It's too much, Em sent to her. *Something is wrong, Kaia!*

Kaia could feel it for herself. The ritual was too powerful, moving too fast, drawing too much from her. She understood then why the other shadowseers who attempted it had died. The ritual had been designed to put out the maximum amount of power to overwhelm the shadows, but that power was too much for any human to contain.

She and Em were going to die.

They couldn't stop the ritual, they couldn't slow it down, and they couldn't keep putting out power at a rate that was burning them up from within, making them both cry out in agony even as their combined powers drove more shadows back into the outer darkness.

Distantly, Kaia realized that she was on her knees, without the strength to rise. She could see the inspector now, on the ground, with blood on his shirt. She could hear Olivia screaming as she fought with another of the shadows. Kaia couldn't do anything to help, though. She couldn't even control the ritual.

There was, she realized, something wrong with it. That knowledge came to her whole and unbidden. The shadow had been in her mind, but in that instant, she knew that she had been in its mind at the same time. And the shadow that had possessed her knew all about the ritual. It had spent lifetimes contemplating it, learning every nuance of it. It understood that power in a way that even the shadowseers barely did.

And because Kaia had shared a mind with it, she had that knowledge now.

It meant that she knew where the ritual was flawed. She knew where she had to change the flow of the power. It wasn't easy now, burning away a mark, replacing it with another. The effort of it felt as if the last iota of Kaia's being were being burned away with it.

She could barely feel her sister now. They weren't something separate. They were only energy, and that energy was burning away, little by little.

Yet she did it. The mark changed, and with it, the whole flow of the ritual shifted.

Now it felt as though Kaia had the power to do what she needed. She reached out for portals around the world, slamming them closed, but that wasn't her main focus. She came back to herself in a fury of power, throwing up a hand toward the portal that hung above the Acropolis.

It strained, bulged, and then tore to shreds in an explosion of dark power that sent a thunderclap sounding across the whole of Athens.

Kaia wasn't done yet, though. She gathered her remaining power, focused it, and then sent it out toward every shadow she could sense, all at once. She ripped them from the bodies of those they possessed like a fisherman yanking on a line, sending them all up to roil and shift in a great mass above her.

Em was there beside her then, and the two of them raised their hands simultaneously.

"This is for our parents," Em said, in a strained voice.

Light blazed out from them, striking the flock of shadows with the power of a thousand suns. It burned them away as surely as morning mist. They made an awful, tearing, roaring sound as the light burned them to nothing, but Kaia didn't relent, didn't hold back for a moment.

The largest of them was the last. It hung above them, throwing darkness down to meet their light, trying to hold them back as it drew dark power from its own world.

"You think you can stop us? You think that I can't destroy you both?"

It flung darkness down at them like a weapon, a spear of piercing cold that seemed to try to leach the life from Kaia and from Em. Kaia understood what it was doing. If it could distract them even for a moment, the ritual would kill them both.

Kaia let out a scream of effort and flung light at it, the power cutting through the darkness, driving into the shadow beyond. It tore at it, ripping the shadow into dark fragments, leaving nothing behind but the sight of the sky beyond.

The orb rose from her hand then, spinning faster and faster until, with a final flare of light, it disintegrated into dust.

Kaia felt the power starting to fade, its task complete. She could no longer feel the shadows and the portals around the world, but she knew that the ritual had done its job.

In that moment, everything hurt. She coughed, and that cough came up with blood. Her head spun, and Kaia couldn't keep her footing anymore. She collapsed to the dais, the last of her strength spent. Em was down there already, lying on her back, her eyes half closed. Kaia reached out weakly for her hand.

The last thing she saw was the sight of the stars up above them both.

CHAPTER TWENTY SEVEN

It was light when Kaia came back to herself, blinking awake in the sunlight streaming through the window of... wait, where was she? She sat bolt upright in bed in a sudden panic, not recognizing the room she was in. It was bright and white painted, with a view from its window out over a broad garden.

Kaia got up, although the first time she tried it she felt so dizzy she had to sit back down again on the edge of the bed. There was a dress laid out for her at its foot; not one of hers, but a cream-colored, floor-length one that looked as if it would fit her well.

It did, and Kaia pulled on her shoes, still looking around warily. What was this? The last thing she remembered... the last she remembered, she and Em had been on the verge of death, doing everything in their power to close the portals and destroy the shadows. The others had been in the midst of a fight against dozens of the possessed.

What had happened to all of them? That question sent a thread of worry through Kaia, so she ran for the door to the room, throwing it open in a rush. Was Em all right? Was the inspector, her aunt, Olivia? Kaia had to know, had to find it out as she ran out onto a landing lined with rooms, which opened out onto a kind of mezzanine balcony over a large central room.

Kaia dared to breathe a sigh of relief as she looked down and saw her aunt, Olivia, and the inspector seated on couches below, all looking bruised but very much alive and well.

She couldn't see Em, though, and that absence sent raw terror running through Kaia.

Em! Em, can you hear me?

It's hard not to, when you shout that loud, her sister complained. A moment or two later, Em came stumbling out of another room along the landing, and Kaia hurried over to throw her arms around her sister.

"I thought you were dead!" Kaia said as she held onto Em.

"Hug me much tighter and you'll suffocate me anyway," Em replied, with a wince. "I'm pretty beaten up, you know."

Kaia stepped back from her sister, looking her over, wanting to make sure that she wasn't seriously hurt. Em must have seen the concern, because she shrugged.

"I'm fine," she said. "How are *you*, Kaia?"

Kaia wasn't sure. She'd thought she was going to die back there in the Acropolis. She'd been ready to give up her life if it stopped the shadows. She hadn't thought beyond that.

Now, she felt tired, raw, and empty. Her whole body felt abused, as if it could barely take everything that had happened to it in the course of the ritual. Her power… it was there when Kaia went looking for it, but it didn't come rushing up through her. After so much exertion, it seemed even that needed to replenish itself a little.

"Are you two going to come down here?" Olivia called out from below, looking up at them when Kaia looked over the balcony. "You've been asleep all night and most of the day."

Kaia found some stairs and hurried down to the large central space. There, Olivia rushed forward to hug her and Em, then led them back to the couches. Their aunt was standing there waiting for them, putting her hands on their shoulders.

"How do you feel, girls?" she asked.

"Like I've been trampled by a horse," Kaia admitted.

"Me too," Em said.

"Good," Aunt Keris said, although she smiled. "It's no less than the two of you deserve for absolutely terrifying me. I thought you were both dead. When we had to carry you down from the Acropolis, I thought… I thought you weren't going to make it."

"I have to second that," the inspector said. He stood and moved to Kaia, putting his hands on her shoulders and holding her out at arm's length. "Thank you for coming to save me, Kaia, but you shouldn't have put yourself at risk. Not for me."

Kaia shook her head. "If I don't put myself in danger for you, who *do* I do it for?"

The inspector meant as much to her as anyone in the world. Kaia might have a mystical connection with her twin, might be able to talk to Em mind to mind, but the inspector meant just as much to her at this point. He was like a father to her.

"And the ritual," Aunt Keris said. "I thought we agreed that you weren't going to undertake the ritual."

"Wait," Em said. "Are we getting scolded for saving the world now?"

"Just a little," Aunt Keris said. "We could have lost you."

"But you didn't," Kaia said. "It worked. At least... I think it worked. Did it work?"

She realized that, while she thought she'd seen the end of all the shadows, the portal closing above her, it might have been a hallucination, or a dream, or something else. It might not have been as complete a destruction as she thought. It might not have worked at all.

"It worked," Olivia said. There was a note of awe in her voice. "It definitely worked. The moment you and Em did... whatever you did, every person there was themselves again. The portal above us closed, and then they were all standing around like they didn't quite know what to do next."

"The question is, do *you* think that it worked?" Aunt Keris said. "The ritual wasn't just designed to close one portal."

Kaia knew what she was asking. She wanted to know if the shadows were truly gone from the world.

"I felt portals all around the world close," she said, and looked across to Em for confirmation. Her sister had been there in the ritual with her. She must have felt everything that Kaia did.

"Dozens of them," Em said. "Maybe more. I *think* it was every one, but I don't know."

"And the shadows?" Inspector Pinsley asked.

"Pushed back through the gates or destroyed," Kaia said. There was a kind of satisfaction to saying that after the shadows had hurt and killed so many people. They had been an implacable enemy to humanity since the days when the ruins of Athens had been brand new, and now... now they were gone, driven back or destroyed.

The sheer enormity of that took a moment or two to settle on her. Kaia knew that there would be no recognition for what she and Em had done, no monuments or awards, but the two of them had just changed the world in a way that Kaia had been told was impossible.

It seemed to sink in with Em in that moment too, because she took Kaia's hand, smiling broadly.

We did it. We actually did it. We beat the shadows!

They had. The only question now was what came next.

Kaia found herself looking around at the grand house around them. It wasn't the place that Cassiopeia had stolen, and it definitely wasn't the shadowseers' safehouse. Marble statues and elegant frescos stood around the walls, while small fruit trees stood in earthenware pots, catching the sun that came in from a great open roof.

"Where are we?" she asked.

"Our host will be back in a moment or two," the inspector said. "He is a magistrate here in Athens."

"A magistrate?" That word made worry return to Kaia's heart. Did that mean... "Are we in trouble for all of this?"

It occurred to her then that the shots fired at the Acropolis would have attracted the attention of whatever police the city had. When they came, what would they have found? Essentially a battleground, with some of the people who had been attacking them while possessed by the shadows wounded or dead.

Was it possible that Kaia and the others were only waiting here until the magistrate came back to declare them all murderers? Certainly, she couldn't see the weapons that her aunt and the inspector had been carrying. Had those been taken from them?

"It's all right, Kaia," the inspector said, and then nodded to a far corner of the courtyard. "Ah, here we are."

A man was coming forward, expensively dressed in formal robes that were presumably those of a magistrate in this city. He was tall, with a dark, curling beard that fell almost to his waist.

He looked vaguely familiar, and it took Kaia a moment or two to realize that he had been there at the Acropolis. He'd been one of the possessed, one of the ones who had grabbed her and held her while the shadow in the inspector had sought to convince her to do what it wanted. The sight of him there like that felt ominous, but even as he approached, the man gave her a broad smile.

"Ah, you are awake!" he said in English as he approached. He held out a hand, clutched Kaia's hand in his, and shook it with such force that Kaia half suspected that her hand was about to be crushed with the enthusiasm of it. He went from her to Em, shaking her hand with just as much vigor.

"We owe you a debt of gratitude," he said. "Both of you."

"I'm sorry," Kaia said, slightly taken aback by it all. "Who are you?"

"My name is Christos Tsimpliades," the man said. "I am a magistrate here in Athens, and until the two of you freed me, I was controlled by one of those vile shadow things."

Kaia knew that part, at least.

"Come, sit down," he said. "We should talk. Are the two of you well? When we carried you back, we did not believe that you were injured, but it is easy to be wrong about these things in such chaos."

He talked with a speed and enthusiasm that Kaia didn't associate with a magistrate. To her, they were big, stern, silent men, but Christos seemed to have an ebullience that was easy to get caught up in.

Kaia sat down on one of the couches, with Em beside her. The inspector and her aunt sat together, and Kaia caught the light brush of their hands against one another. Olivia perched on the edge of a chair to one side.

"I imagine the two of you have questions about what happened after you fell unconscious," the magistrate said.

Kaia nodded. She still didn't know what had happened in the aftermath of it all.

"Obviously, I saw you collapse. I and the others around me were suddenly free of the things that had been in us, suddenly standing in the midst of what seemed like a battleground, trying to make sense of it all. There were people hurt. There were people who had been killed in the fighting."

That fact made Kaia wince. The thought of people dying because the shadows had thrown them into combat against the people she loved was slightly sickening. It wasn't their fault that they'd been made to fight, but when they'd come at her and the others, there had been no choice but to fight back.

Kaia found herself wondering if she had hurt anyone in that fighting. She had flung people back with her powers; what if one of them had landed badly, or slammed into a pillar hard enough to snap their neck? The thought that Kaia might have killed someone was almost too much to bear.

"Are we in trouble for that fight?" Em asked, obviously thinking about the same thing, but from a different angle.

"That is what I have just been away talking to people about," Christos said. "We are all lucky in one way: many of the people who were... not in control of themselves up there are important people. Powerful people."

Kaia nodded. Having control of people like that had allowed the shadows to do what they wanted in the city without anyone interfering.

She frowned then. "Wait. If powerful people were hurt and killed..."

"The whole thing has been blamed on a bout of collective madness, brought on by bad vapors in the air," Christos said. "Those vapors then caught light, burning them away in a sudden flash."

Kaia thought of the explosive burst of her and Em's powers out around the Acropolis.

"Will people actually believe that?" Olivia asked.

Christos shrugged. "What matters is that there is an explanation, not that it is a good one. Too many important people now have a vested interest in going along with that explanation."

"So there will be no issues for us?" the inspector asked, in a serious tone. He was obviously worried about protecting Kaia and the others from any legal ramifications of all of this.

"None," Christos assured him. "You think we'll arrest you? We're *grateful* to you for all you've done."

"And the man who accosted me on the way up to the Acropolis?" Pinsley asked.

"What man?" Kaia said.

The inspector looked over to her. "A Mr. Illingworth, an investigator from London."

The man who had questioned Kaia and the others. The one who had been following her last night.

"You say he fell from the slope?" Christos said. He shook his head. "A man could not survive such a fall, but there are no signs of his remains. With no body, I doubt that there will be any more questions."

Kaia felt a sense of relief at that. The inspector had already been hunted by bounty hunters over Europe. She didn't want him facing more trouble with the law now.

Christos's expression turned more serious, and Kaia knew then that not all of the news would be good.

"Unfortunately, I do have one unwelcome matter to discuss. Now that the young ladies have recovered, I must ask you all to leave Athens."

"What?" Olivia said. "Why?"

It seemed that Aunt Keris understood, though. "The same important people who are making sure that there are no consequences for the events of last night do not want a reminder of an alternate version of events in their city. With the shadows gone, we are the last traces of the uncanny left here, and they want us gone."

The magistrate had the grace to look a little embarrassed, at least. "I fear so. It need not be immediate, though, and I will assist your return to England in any way I may. I will leave you to discuss it, my friends."

He walked off, presumably to deal with more of the details involved in covering up the events of the previous night. It left Kaia with more questions than answers.

"*Are* we going back to London?" she asked. "*Can* we go back to London?"

If Superintendent Hutton had sent men to chase down the inspector, then what would happen if Inspector Pinsley returned of his own accord? Would there be policemen waiting to arrest him?

"There might be problems with my adoptive father too," Em pointed out. "As far as the British Ambassador to France is concerned, his daughter has run off with a group of strangers involved in causing chaos in Paris. I... I want to see him again, but I'm worried about the kind of trouble there will be when I do."

In that moment, their victory didn't seem quite so complete. They had beaten the shadows, but apparently all that had earned them was to be sent away, unable to go home, without anywhere really that they could go next.

"We will find somewhere to go," Aunt Keris said. "Shadowseers are resourceful. Wherever we end up, we will make it into a home. Perhaps we could head to the Americas, or to one of the further reaches of the British Empire?"

"I do not believe that will be necessary," the inspector said. "I think we should all return to London."

"But you'll be arrested!" Kaia said.

The inspector shook his head. "Perhaps a day ago, yes, but now..."

He took something out of the pocket of the linen coat he was wearing. It was a thick leather-bound notebook, which looked as though someone had carried it around with them for years.

"This ledger belonged to the man who sought to kill me up by the Acropolis," Inspector Pinsley said. "I had heard that Mr. Frederick Illingworth was a man who collected secrets, so when I found it, I took the time to read through it."

Kaia glanced at the pages. The squiggles there had nothing to do with any letters she knew.

"It's in code," Em said, also looking.

"It is," the inspector said. "A most ingenious cipher. It took me several hours to crack."

"You can read all that?" Olivia asked.

"Mr. Illingworth was not *quite* as clever as he wished to believe," the inspector said. "Although he was certainly cunning enough to collect a wealth of secrets about a wide variety of powerful individuals. I believe that, were it to be known that I had access to such secrets, and that they would be revealed if I were arrested, I might be left quite carefully alone."

"Blackmail, Sebastian?" Aunt Keris said. "I doubt anyone would believe that the upright Inspector Pinsley would resort to such a thing."

"They already think I have caused chaos across half the continent," the inspector said. "I think they will believe this part too."

"What does that mean?" Kaia asked.

The inspector smiled. "It means that we're going home."

CHAPTER TWENTY EIGHT

London was, Kaia had to admit, beautiful in its own way. She'd been back months now, and the beauty of it didn't fade. She had seen the reworked elegance of Paris, the old-fashioned charm of Munich, the grandeur of Rome, and the classical remains of Athens, but there was something about London that stuck with her.

Maybe it was just that it was where home was.

Home, in this case, was a large town house off Grosvenor Square, the kind of place Kaia could never have imagined living when she was growing up in the orphanage, except perhaps as a servant. It was certainly never the kind of place where she might have imagined herself being *happy*.

Now, she ran up the steps to the large, dark front door and let herself in. The moment she did, she heard the sound of the usual joyous chaos of the place.

"Em, Em, calm down, it's fine," Olivia said.

"Calm down? This dress isn't right at all. I have to go change!"

Her sister rushed out from the drawing room, then ran up the broad staircase toward the bedrooms. Although she was still technically the ward of the now former British Ambassador to France, she still had her own room here with the rest of them, kept in a perpetual state of disarray that Kaia suspected only Em truly understood.

"Hi, Em," Kaia called out after her.

No time! I have to get ready!

Olivia came out of the drawing room, smiling at Kaia as she looked up the stairs to see where Em had gone.

"Is Casper coming over?" Kaia asked. It was the only thing she could think of that might have Em so flustered.

"Yes," Olivia replied, obviously enjoying herself. "I believe he wants to take her to the fair on Clapham Common. I'll be chaperoning."

"Your father insisted?"

"He's almost amusingly overprotective," Olivia said. "Personally, I think that if a boy is prepared to follow Em back all the way across Europe, we should allow the two of them a little space. Em is sensible enough."

Kaia frowned slightly at that.

"All right, maybe sensible isn't the right word," Olivia admitted. "Would you like to come?"

Kaia shook her head. The fair sounded fun, but she didn't want to get in her sister's way for this.

As she thought it, a door at the end of the hall opened, letting out the inspector and a shorter man expensively dressed in breeches, long coat, and top hat.

"Thank you again for your help, Mr. Pinsley. You have the gratitude of her majesty's government. You're *sure* this will work, though?"

"I have every confidence, Minister."

The expensively dressed man tipped his hat to Olivia and Kaia as he passed, then left.

"Wasn't that the Home Secretary?" Olivia asked her father.

He was still the inspector in Kaia's mind in spite of being let go from the police almost as soon as they returned. Well, no. He'd been *arrested* as soon as they returned, but that hadn't lasted long. As he'd guessed, the secrets in Mr. Illingworth's notebook had been more than enough to get him released.

"I was just helping him with a small matter," the inspector said. "Nothing too taxing."

The days now seemed to be filled with small matters, with people coming to the door to ask the inspector for help. Some were important people, government ministers, members of parliament or the House of Lords, wealthy members of the aristocracy. Others were normal residents of the city, coming with small problems, people who had gone missing, mysteries that the police wouldn't or couldn't solve.

"Shall we go through?" the inspector said. "I believe Keris is waiting for us in the dining room."

Their aunt was indeed there, sitting at a long dining table with brunch set out in front of her. She was sitting reading the latest broadsheets, making notes as she went, as she usually did. She stood as they all came in, moving over to kiss the inspector, her wedding ring catching the light.

She hugged Kaia next. "How were things over at St Michael's?"

"The rebuilding on the windows is almost complete," Kaia said. "Lottie has finished a couple of new art pieces, and Reverend Faulkner is talking about handing out food in some of the poorest parts of the city."

"Ah, so things are trundling along as usual?" the inspector said.

"Pretty much," Kaia said.

There was something wonderful about being able to just sit down and do something normal with the people she loved, here in the house they'd bought in London using some of Mr. Illingworth's ill-gotten gains.

"I take it everything went well with the minister?" Aunt Keris said. "You've managed to locate the would-be traitor?"

That was the inspector's idea of a small matter? It probably said a lot about their lives that it probably *did* count as small.

"It didn't take much," the inspector said. "The man left a trail that was easy enough to reason out, once I had all the facts. Have *you* found anything, dear?"

"One or two things," Aunt Keris said. "Oh, the broadsheets are full of the usual rubbish, but there have been a couple of interesting letters. A man who believes his house is full of ghosts, and a village where girls appear to be going missing, along with rumors of fairy rings and the fey."

"Both potentially just stories," the inspector pointed out.

"But we're going to look into them, right?" Kaia asked. She emphasized the "we." This was one side of the family's investigation business that she was determined to be a part of.

"Of course we're going to look into them," Aunt Keris said. "I have already arranged the railway tickets."

That was good. Kaia loved the fact that they all had a normal life here, that she had a family at last. Normal was good, but she and the others weren't going to stop investigating, weren't going to stop looking into the uncanny and fighting any last vestiges of the shadows where they arose.

Maybe one day there would be another great threat from those shadows. For now, though, there were smaller mysteries to solve.

It was more than enough.

NOW AVAILABLE!

REALM OF DRAGONS
(Age of the Sorcerers—Book One)

"Has all the ingredients for an instant success: plots, counterplots, mystery, valiant knights, and blossoming relationships replete with broken hearts, deception and betrayal. It will keep you entertained for hours, and will satisfy all ages. Recommended for the permanent library of all fantasy readers."
--Books and Movie Reviews, Roberto Mattos (re *The Sorcerer's Ring*)

"The beginnings of something remarkable are there."
--San Francisco Book Review (re *A Quest of Heroes*)

From USA Today and #1 bestseller Morgan Rice, author of *A Quest of Heroes* (over 1,300 five star reviews) comes the debut of a startlingly new fantasy series.

REALM OF DRAGONS (Age of the Sorcerers—Book One) tells the story of the epic coming of age of one very special 16 year old boy, a blacksmith's son from a poor family who is offered no chance of proving his fighting skills and breaking into the ranks of the nobles. Yet he holds a power he cannot deny, and a fate he must follow.

It tells the story of a 17 year old princess on the eve of her wedding, destined for greatness—and of her younger sister, rejected by her family and dying of plague.

It tells the tale of their three brothers, three princes who could not be more different from each other—all of them vying for power.

It tells the story of a kingdom on the verge of change, of invasion, the story of the dying dragon race, falling daily from the sky.

It tells the tale of two rival kingdoms, of the rapids dividing them, of a landscape dotted with dormant volcanoes, and of a capital accessible only with the tides. It is a story of love, passion, of hate and sibling rivalry; of rogues and hidden treasure; of monks and secret warriors; of honor and glory, and of betrayal and deception.

It is the story of Dragonfell, a story of honor and valor, of sorcerers, magic, fate and destiny. It is a tale you will not put down until the early hours, one that will transport you to another world and have you fall in in love with characters you will never forget. It appeals to all ages and genders.

Books #2-#8 are also available!

"A spirited fantasy ....Only the beginning of what promises to be an epic young adult series."
--Midwest Book Review (re *A Quest of Heroes*)

"Action-packed .... Rice's writing is solid and the premise intriguing."
--Publishers Weekly (re *A Quest of Heroes*)

Books by Morgan Rice

SHADOWSEER
SHADOWDEER: LONDON (Book #1)
SHADOWSEER: PARIS (Book #2)
SHADOWSEER: MUNICH (Book #3)
SHADOWSEER: ROME (Book #4)
SHADOWSEER: ATHENS (Book #5)

AGE OF THE SORCERERS
REALM OF DRAGONS (Book #1)
THRONE OF DRAGONS (Book #2)
BORN OF DRAGONS (Book #3)
RING OF DRAGONS (Book #4)
CROWN OF DRAGONS (Book #5)
DUSK OF DRAGONS (Book #6)
SHIELD OF DRAGONS (Book #7)
DREAM OF DRAGONS (Book #8)

OLIVER BLUE AND THE SCHOOL FOR SEERS
THE MAGIC FACTORY (Book #1)
THE ORB OF KANDRA (Book #2)
THE OBSIDIANS (Book #3)
THE SCEPTOR OF FIRE (Book #4)

THE INVASION CHRONICLES
TRANSMISSION (Book #1)
ARRIVAL (Book #2)
ASCENT (Book #3)
RETURN (Book #4)

THE WAY OF STEEL
ONLY THE WORTHY (Book #1)
ONLY THE VALIANT (Book #2)
ONLY THE DESTINED (Book #3)
ONLY THE BOLD (Book #4)

A THRONE FOR SISTERS
A THRONE FOR SISTERS (Book #1)
A COURT FOR THIEVES (Book #2)
A SONG FOR ORPHANS (Book #3)
A DIRGE FOR PRINCES (Book #4)
A JEWEL FOR ROYALS (BOOK #5)
A KISS FOR QUEENS (BOOK #6)
A CROWN FOR ASSASSINS (Book #7)
A CLASP FOR HEIRS (Book #8)

OF CROWNS AND GLORY
SLAVE, WARRIOR, QUEEN (Book #1)
ROGUE, PRISONER, PRINCESS (Book #2)
KNIGHT, HEIR, PRINCE (Book #3)
REBEL, PAWN, KING (Book #4)
SOLDIER, BROTHER, SORCERER (Book #5)
HERO, TRAITOR, DAUGHTER (Book #6)
RULER, RIVAL, EXILE (Book #7)
VICTOR, VANQUISHED, SON (Book #8)

KINGS AND SORCERERS
RISE OF THE DRAGONS (Book #1)
RISE OF THE VALIANT (Book #2)
THE WEIGHT OF HONOR (Book #3)
A FORGE OF VALOR (Book #4)
A REALM OF SHADOWS (Book #5)
NIGHT OF THE BOLD (Book #6)

THE SORCERER'S RING
A QUEST OF HEROES (Book #1)
A MARCH OF KINGS (Book #2)
A FATE OF DRAGONS (Book #3)
A CRY OF HONOR (Book #4)
A VOW OF GLORY (Book #5)
A CHARGE OF VALOR (Book #6)
A RITE OF SWORDS (Book #7)
A GRANT OF ARMS (Book #8)
A SKY OF SPELLS (Book #9)
A SEA OF SHIELDS (Book #10)
A REIGN OF STEEL (Book #11)

A LAND OF FIRE (Book #12)
A RULE OF QUEENS (Book #13)
AN OATH OF BROTHERS (Book #14)
A DREAM OF MORTALS (Book #15)
A JOUST OF KNIGHTS (Book #16)
THE GIFT OF BATTLE (Book #17)

THE SURVIVAL TRILOGY
ARENA ONE: SLAVERSUNNERS (Book #1)
ARENA TWO (Book #2)
ARENA THREE (Book #3)

VAMPIRE, FALLEN
BEFORE DAWN (Book #1)

THE VAMPIRE JOURNALS
TURNED (Book #1)
LOVED (Book #2)
BETRAYED (Book #3)
DESTINED (Book #4)
DESIRED (Book #5)
BETROTHED (Book #6)
VOWED (Book #7)
FOUND (Book #8)
RESURRECTED (Book #9)
CRAVED (Book #10)
FATED (Book #11)
OBSESSED (Book #12)

About Morgan Rice

Morgan Rice is the #1 bestselling and USA Today bestselling author of the epic fantasy series THE SORCERER'S RING, comprising seventeen books; of the #1 bestselling series THE VAMPIRE JOURNALS, comprising twelve books; of the #1 bestselling series THE SURVIVAL TRILOGY, a post-apocalyptic thriller comprising three books; of the epic fantasy series KINGS AND SORCERERS, comprising six books; of the epic fantasy series OF CROWNS AND GLORY, comprising eight books; of the epic fantasy series A THRONE FOR SISTERS, comprising eight books; of the science fiction series THE INVASION CHRONICLES, comprising four books; of the fantasy series OLIVER BLUE AND THE SCHOOL FOR SEERS, comprising four books; of the fantasy series THE WAY OF STEEL, comprising four books; of the fantasy series AGE OF THE SORCERERS, comprising eight books; and of the new fantasy series SHADOWSEER, comprising five books. Morgan's books are available in audio and print editions, and translations are available in over 25 languages.

Morgan loves to hear from you, so please feel free to visit www.morganricebooks.com to join the email list, receive a free book, receive free giveaways, download the free app, get the latest exclusive news, connect on Facebook and Twitter, and stay in touch!